Published by BSA Publishing 2020 who

assert the right that no part of this

publication may be reproduced, stored in

a retrieval system or transmitted by any

means without the prior permission of the

publishers.

Proof read/editing by Zeldos

Cover art by Impact Print, Hereford

1

The author acknowledges the help and advice received from Ian Kennedy at the British Association of Rose Breeders in writing this book.

All available as individual or double 'case' e-books and paperbacks.

LONDON CRIME   1930s-present day.

An in-depth look at the geezers, the gangs and the heists. Includes the Brinks Mat Robbery, Great Train Robbery, Baker Street and Princess Margaret Photos robbery, Hatton Garden and much, much more.

THE PALMER CASES BACKGROUND

Justin Palmer started off on the beat as a London policeman in the late 1980s and is now Detective Chief Superintendent Palmer running the Serial Murder Squad from New Scotland Yard.

Not one to pull punches, or give a hoot for political correctness if it hinders his enquiries Palmer has gone as far as he will go in the Met. and he knows it. Master of the one line put down and slave to his sciatica he can be as nasty or as nice as he likes.

The early 2000's was a time of re-awakening for Palmer as the Information Technology revolution turned forensic science, communication and information gathering skills upside down. In 2012 realising the value of this revolution to crime solving Palmer co-opted Detective Sergeant

Gheeta Singh, a British Asian, working in the Met's Cyber Crime Unit onto his team. DS Singh has a degree in IT and was given the go ahead to update Palmer's department with all the computer hard and software she wanted, most of which she wrote herself, and some of which is, shall we say, of a grey area when it comes to privacy laws and accessing certain databases!

Together with their civilian computer clerk called Claire, nicknamed 'JCB' by the team because she keeps on digging, they take on the serial killers of the UK. If more help is needed in a case Gheeta calls on a select number of officers in other departments who have worked with Palmer before and can't wait to do so again.

On the personal front Palmer has been married to his 'princess', or Mrs P. as she is known to everybody, for nearly thirty years. The romance blossomed after the young DC Palmer arrested most of her family who were a bunch of South London petty villains in the 90's. They have a nice house in Dulwich Village and a faithful dog called Daisy. His one nemesis is his next door neighbour Benji, real name Benjamin Courtney-Smith, a portly, single, ex-advertising executive in his late fifties who has taken early retirement and now had, in Palmer's estimation, too much time on his hands and too much money in his pocket. A new car every year plus at least two cruise holidays a year to exotic parts; he wears designer label clothes befitting a much younger man, a fake tan, enough gold jewellery to interest the Hatton Garden Safe Deposit Heist gang and all topped off with his thinning hair scooped into a ponytail also befitting a much younger man. Benji has a habit of bringing calamities into Palmer's settled home life.

Palmer is also unsure about Benji's sexuality, as his mincing walk and the very female way of flapping his hands to illustrate every word cast doubts in Palmer's mind. Not that that worries Palmer, who is quite at ease in the multi-gender world of today. Of course, he will never admit it, but the main grudge he holds against Benji is that before his arrival in the quiet suburb of Dulwich village, Palmer had been the favourite amongst the ladies of the Women's Institute, the Bridge Club, the Church Flower Arrangers and the various other clubs catering for ladies of a certain age; but now Benji has usurped Palmer's fan base, and when he stood for and was elected to the local council on a mandate to reopen the library and bring back the free bus pass for pensioners Benji's popularity soared and their fluttering eyelashes had turned away from Palmer and settled in his direction.   Gheeta Singh, Palmer's DS and number two is twenty six and lives in a fourth floor Barbican apartment in London. Her parents arrived on these shores as refugees fleeing from Idi Amin's Uganda in the 1970's. Her father and brothers have built up a large computer parts supply company in which it was assumed Gheeta would take an active role on graduating from University with her IT degrees. However she had other ideas on her career path, and also on the arranged marriage her mother and aunt still try to coerce her into. Gheeta has two loves, police work and technology, and thanks to Palmer she has her dream job.

Combining the old 'coppers nose' and 'gut feelings' of Palmer with the modern IT skills of DS Singh the two make an unlikely but successful crime solving pair. As the name of the squad suggests, all their cases involve serial killings and twist and turn through red herrings and hidden clues alike, hopefully keeping the reader in suspense until the very end.

THE BLACK ROSE

WEDNESDAY

'He looks like he's sleeping, I can't see any wounds.'

DCS Justin Palmer moved around the steel trolley in the morgue to look at the rest of the male body laid out on it. The only 'wound' was the closed incision Professor Latin the pathologist had made for the post-mortem so he could remove the inner organs for weighing and examination. Palmer had taken Latin's call earlier that day and together with DS Gheeta Singh had made the journey across the river from the Yard to the morgue at Latin's request. As usual when visiting Latin with a female officer, Palmer had apologised before entering the morgue for Latin's well known use of expletives. It wasn't often that Latin called in Palmer, so something unusual must have caught his attention. The Murder Squad morgue was not a place Palmer was keen on visiting, as the smell of dead flesh, formaldehyde and disinfectant has a habit of clinging to clothes, and even though he and DS Singh were in regulation white overalls plus hair and shoe coverings, Mrs P. would know as soon as he got home that evening that he'd been to the morgue, and would insist his clothes went into the wash and he went into the shower. Palmer looked around. No, it wasn't a very nice place. The four latest gang stabbing victims from the weekend's London drug wars were laid out on other benches, plastic sheets covering their bodies. Palmer guessed they'd all be young men in their teens or early twenties, lured into selling drugs by the promise of easy money. It didn't work that way. His attention was brought back to his own case by Professor Latin.

'There are no fucking wounds,' Latin said. He pointed across the morgue to another trolley carrying a middle-aged lady. 'None on her either. She's the wife, he's the husband – both found in the back of their family business Transit van parked at the back of the lorry park at South Mimms Services off the M25 three days ago. All dead, with a pipe attached to the exhaust and poked into the van through a floor drainage plug hole'

'A floor drainage plug hole?'

'The family business was a garden centre, the van would have been used to carry plants about. Plants need watering, hence the drainage hole.'

'So it's a family suicide then?' Palmer knew it wouldn't be. Latin wouldn't have called him out to the morgue for straightforward suicides.

'No, a fucking family *murder*.' Latin gave Palmer a beaming smile.

'Do we know who they are?' Palmer asked DS Singh, who stood nearby and had her laptop open and fired up. She was well used to Latin's language, which was nothing more than you'd hear in the Yard's canteen every day and was like water off a duck's back to her.

'The Hanleys, guv,' she read off the screen. 'According to the report from the local station the deceased are Geoffrey and Linda Hanley. Geoffrey Hanley has a garden centre business in Borehamwood. No other family members and no previous dealings with the police – they seem to be just an ordinary pair.'

'No children?'

'No, not according to BDM records. I checked.'

Palmer turned back to Latin. 'So it's a murder not a suicide then, is it? Go on, explain.'

'Well, the first thing I noticed was an abnormal reading from the lungs. The toxicology test on his lungs showed no residue of CO or NO2. Same test on the female gave the same reading, no CO or NO2.'

Palmer spread his hands. 'Which are?'

'Carbon monoxide and nitrogen dioxide, the stuff that makes up most of car exhaust fumes and pollutes our streets.'

'Neither of them had any of that stuff in their lungs?' Palmer looked from one body to the other. 'A bit strange if they died by inhaling it from a pipe run from the exhaust.'

'There were very small traces, but we all have that in our lungs – can't avoid it if you live in or near a city or town. But they certainly didn't inhale enough to kill them, no way.'

'And no wounds on the bodies either, no bruises or strangulation marks?'

'None.' Latin shook his head in an exaggerated manner to underline the point. 'None at all.'

Having worked with Professor Latin for many years, Palmer was well aware of his theatrical approach to post mortems; Latin knew perfectly well what had caused the Hanley's deaths, and was making Palmer wait for the final reveal like a Poirot final chapter twist. Palmer rolled his eyes at Gheeta, who was well aware of Latin's ways as well.

'So how did they die?'

'Poison.'

'Poison?'

'Yes.' Silence.

Palmer's patience was waning. 'Are you going to explain what happened to these people, or are we going to proceed one word at a time? I've got Mrs P.'s steak and kidney pie for dinner tonight, and at the rate you're going it'll be cold or in the dog by the time I get home.'

Latin took the hint. 'Because the bodies exhibited a lack of exhaust fume damage to the lungs, we examined all the organs and stomach contents thoroughly. In the stomachs of both deceased we found traces of the poison wolfsbane, which comes from the root of the deadly aconitum family of plants; a very pretty and popular plant you can buy at most garden centres. As are many plants with deadly poison attributes, like digitalis, belladonna and others.'

'What do you mean *it comes from the root*? Are you saying the Hanleys sat in the van and ate the root of a plant to kill themselves?'

'No, not at all the root has to be dried and crushed first, but it could then be put in a drink or on food – it's tasteless.'

'Hold on a minute, I'm getting confused. They were found in the back of their company van with the exhaust pipe pushed through, but were actually killed by this wolfsbane poison?'

'Yes.'

Gheeta interrupted as she read from her screen. 'No cups or drinking vessels found in the van, guv. It was completely empty in the back except for the bodies, fully clothed.'

'Where are the clothes?

'Forensics have them.'

'They were dead before they were put in that van,' said Latin forcibly, a little annoyed that the spotlight had been taken off him.

'They were? How do you know that?' Palmer asked.

'The amount of wolfsbane in their bloodstream and stomach indicates a very quick death. That poison paralyses the body's organs and overpowers the heart – the amount they took would have killed them within two minutes at the most. There's no way either of them could have driven that van after taking the poison.'

'And no cups or anything else in the van, so somebody else poisoned them, put them in the van, dumped it at South Mimms and fed the exhaust through to make it look like suicide.'

'That's for you to find out, Justin. All I can positively say is that it was the poison that killed them, not the exhaust,' said Latin, with all the solemnity of an actor delivering the final revealing line of a play. All that was missing was the sweeping bow at the end.

Palmer half expected all the bodies in the morgue to sit up and applaud.

****

'He gets worse every time I see him.' Palmer and Gheeta were in the back of the squad car outside the morgue. 'I'm surprised he hasn't had a stage put up in the morgue to make his pronouncements from.'

Gheeta was more interested in the local police report on the Hanleys than Latin's theatricals.

'If the family had no next of kin or relatives nobody will know they are dead, guv. There's nothing in the report to say their house or business has been visited by officers, or that anybody has made enquiries about them.'

'Strange, after three days you would think people at their business would be wondering where they were by now.'

Gheeta showed him a picture on her laptop. 'That's the garden centre, looks a nice place, quite big too. Just off the high street in Borehamwood.'

'Okay, let's go and take a look. Get onto the local force involved, speak to the OIC and have him or her transfer the case to us. And tell him or her to keep that information quiet too, if any local media gets wind of the Serial Murder Squad being involved they'll start getting interested, and I don't want that just yet. Then give Claire a call at the Team Room and ask her to contact the motorway services and get copies of their CCTV recordings from the time the van arrived; and then get her digging into the Hanley's background, see if we can't come up with somebody harbouring a grudge big enough to kill for.'

'To kill two people for, guv.'

'Yes, bit like the Mary Celeste isn't it.'

'There weren't any bodies on the Mary Celeste, guv. It was empty.'

'Okay, the Titanic then.'

'No icebergs in Borehamwood, guv.'

Palmer searched for a retort but couldn't think of one.

'Clever arse.' That would do.

Gheeta smiled as she leaned forward and gave the driver the postcode of Hanley's garden centre.

****

'Looks busy doesn't it?' Palmer remarked as they drove off the main road onto the large car park at Hanley's Garden Centre. 'Park at the back, driver, don't want the Sergeant's uniform to frighten the natives.'

Once parked Palmer and Gheeta skirted the perimeter of the car park round to the centre's entrance, getting a few funny looks from shoppers on the way. Inside they found themselves in a very large glass house with rows and rows of benches laden with flower and vegetable plants and gardening requisites of all kinds; it was very tidy with soft classical music piped through the sound system.

'Better make ourselves known.' Palmer walked over to a lady assistant wearing a green company uniform with Hanley's embroidered on the front and back of the jacket. He showed his ID card. 'Hello. Nothing to worry about, just a routine call, but could you point us in the direction of the manager?'

The assistant's immediate minor panic attack at being confronted by police officers holding ID cards diffused as Palmer gave her his killer smile, the one Mrs P. had said could melt the Arctic – well, what's left of it – she relaxed and looked around trying to locate somebody. 'You want Jim, Jim Riley – he's not in here so probably out on the patio. We had some fruit trees come in earlier so I expect he's sorting them out.' She pointed to the back of the premises. 'Through the big doors at the back. If he's not there the office is out there on the left, big wooden shed – he'll be in there.'

Palmer thanked her and they made their way to the back of the glass house and through the big doors into a large open patio beyond where another large glass house loomed. Jim Riley was indeed sorting the fruit trees on the patio; he was struggling with a large potted conference pear, wiggling it into position in line with others and hadn't seen Palmer and Singh approach. Palmer waited until Riley straightened up, panting a bit with the exertion.

'Mister Riley?'

He was young, Gheeta estimated his age as early thirties, and he looked fit, but then if you were manhandling large pots of trees about all day you'd be fit too. Dark hair cut close and a face that had a chiselled appearance – all in all Gheeta thought Jim Riley to be quite handsome.

Riley was taken aback by Palmer's ID card and Gheeta's uniform. 'Yes, that's me. What can I do for you.'

Palmer flashed his fatherly smile this time, 'Nothing to worry yourself about, Mister Riley. Is there somewhere private we could go?'

'Yes, yes the office.' He pointed to the large shed on the side of the patio the assistant had mentioned and walked towards it, taking a key from his pocket and opening the door.

Inside was a bit of a mess; an old table that might be more at home at the local tip held centre stage, with a chair behind it and two in front that both Palmer and Gheeta felt inclined not to trust despite Riley offering them.

'Sit down, sit down please.'

'That's all right sir, I'll stand if you don't mind. Been sitting in a car all day,' lied Palmer, eyeing the chairs. 'I am afraid we have some bad news for you concerning the Hanleys.'

It was noticeable that the blood drained from Riley's face. He didn't speak, so Palmer carried on.

'Can you tell me when you last spoke to them?'

'Yes, yes, four days ago – they were going off on holiday the next day. Why, what's happened?'

'Where were they going for the holiday, sir?'

'Err, Scotland I believe. They often went there, hired a motor home and just toured. What's happened?'

'Well, there seems to have been an accident. I'm sorry to tell you that both Mr and Mrs Hanley are dead.'

Riley looked like Tyson Fury had punched his stomach; his mouth dropped open and he didn't speak for some time. Palmer and Gheeta noted his reaction – it was genuine. Or was it?

'Dead? How?'

'Well it's all a bit perplexing actually.' Palmer took a deep breath. 'They were found in the back of the Hanley Garden Centre Transit van parked at a motorway services, with the exhaust run into the van.'

'What?' Riley's reaction was disbelief. 'Suicide? No, no way.'

Palmer shrugged; he was keeping his cards close to his chest for the time being. 'Well it looks that way at present sir, but we have to wait for the post mortems. Can you think of any reason why they should take their own lives, if indeed that's what has happened – money troubles, family rows?'

Riley was regaining his composure, 'No, no not at all – no rows anyway. I don't know anything about the money, we have a bookkeeper in once a week who handles all that side – she does the books, wages and banking.' He pointed to a large solid safe in the corner. 'Daily takings are kept in there and she puts it all together; does the book work and wage packets, and we go to the bank together to put in the rest.'

'Are the books in there too?' asked Gheeta, nodding towards the safe which she was sure Palmer and his lock picks could open in a couple of minutes; a long career in dealing with criminals of all types had given Palmer a few extra skills.

'No.' Riley turned in his chair and pointed at a lever arch file on the shelf behind him. 'It's all in there, daily till receipts books and all that stuff. I put everything in that and she sorts it.'

Gheeta walked round the desk and picked up the file. 'I'll take it for our forensic accountant to take a peek at, just to make sure there weren't money troubles acting on the family's minds.'

'Yes, yes okay.'

'And do you have the bookkeeper's name and number? I'll give them a call.'

'It's only one lady, Alison. Her card's in my drawer.'

He opened a desk drawer and rummaged out a business card which Gheeta took.

Riley was regaining his composure after the initial shock at the news. 'What should I do now, close the centre? It's the Chelsea Flower Show on Sunday – business rockets after that, it's our busiest time. We've stocked up already, so if we close the stock will wilt and die, and so will the business.'

Palmer didn't want that; in fact that was the last thing he wanted. To close the business would put a stop on the one place that might hold the answer to why two people are murdered in a van at a motorway services with it made to look like suicide.

'No, no need to close. I'm sure you can run the day-to-day business of the garden centre and ask the bookkeeper to carry on keeping things in order financially. What I will do is have a word with the bank and explain the situation, banks are usually okay in emergency situations like this. Do you pay the staff in cash?'

'Yes, Alison sorts that out.'

'Good, then carry on as normal for the time being, and one thing I would ask is that you keep this to yourself. If you tell the staff what has happened it won't be very long before the local newspaper gets to know and then you'll be pestered all day long.'

'No, no I don't want that – no, not at all. The staff think they are on holiday so best if I keep it like that, don't you think?'

'Yes I do. Good, okay Mr Riley, I think that's all we can do for the present. My sergeant will give you a direct line to our office, use it if you need us – other than that we will be in touch as soon as we have more information, so for now carry on as before if you would. Now all we need is the address of the company solicitors if you have it? They will do a search just in case there is another director or silent partner we need to talk to.'

Riley nodded. 'I think that will be in here.' He pulled a large desk diary off the shelf behind him and leafed through it. 'Yes, here we are – Michael Whitley, Whitley Solicitors, 28 High Street, Watford.'

Gheeta tapped the address into her laptop.

Now,' Palmer continued as Gheeta passed her direct line card to Riley, 'Is there a back way out that we might take? A police uniform can be guaranteed to start tongues wagging and people getting the wrong idea.'

'Yes, yes follow me – we have a side path that takes you to a staff door into the car park.' He led them out of the office.

'Do you have any aconite plants?' asked Gheeta in an offhand way. 'My mother was looking for some online, apparently they are very pretty and ideal for a hanging basket.'

Jim grimaced, 'Aconite? Yes, but I wouldn't recommend them if there's pets around. They're poisonous, best keep away from them.'

Gheeta feigned surprise, 'Oh really? Right, we won't be buying those then – mum dotes on her cat.'

****

'I'm not sure about him, are you?' Palmer asked Gheeta as they settled back into the squad car.

'No. He seemed genuinely shocked by the news, but not as shocked as he ought to be – after all, it could be his career down the pan if the place closes.'

'Another one for Claire to take a good look at. Where's the Transit van now?'

'Secure pound at Paddington, guv.'

'Email Reg Frome to go and give it a forensic deep clean, see if we can't turn up some clue as to who drove it to the Services with two bodies in the back; and ask him to put a team into the Hanley's home and look for aconite, or anything that might make a man who seems perfectly at ease with the world suddenly commit suicide with his wife. Not that suicide is the main suspicion here.'

Reg Frome led the specialist Murder Squad Forensics team and as such worked with Palmer on most of his cases. They had both started their police careers in the same intake at Hendon College as teenagers, and whilst Palmer opted for the usual career path through the ranks in CID Frome had branched off into the science of forensics, where he had reached the equivalent high office as Palmer. You couldn't miss him; his shock of white hair stood out, making him look a lot like 'Doc' Brown from the *Back To The Future* films.

'Right, next stop the bookkeeper, Alison. Where do we find her?'

'Alison Burnley,' said Gheeta, reading from the card Riley had given her. 'Office is off the high street in Watford.' She passed the card forward to the driver who put the postcode in the SatNav.

****

Jim Riley sat for some minutes contemplating things before pulling out his mobile and speed dialling.

A female voice answered. 'Hello Jim.'

'What have you done?'

'What have I done? What are you talking about?'

'You know what I'm talking about. The Hanleys – what the hell have you done?'

'Jim, I really don't know what you are talking about.'

'Liar. They're dead – both of them, dead.'

There was a silence on the line for a few seconds.

'Hang up Jim, we will come and see you at home tonight.'

Click. The line went dead.

****

Alison Burnley's office, if that is the right name for it, was a small single room at the top of a steep flight of narrow wooden stairs that led off the high street in Watford beside an Indian takeaway.

Palmer eyed the stairs with worry; his sciatica had a habit of letting him know its presence when climbing stairs, especially steep ones. He motioned Gheeta to go first and took his time going up behind her. A knock on the old wooden door that had a bevelled glass panel that showed its age around the cheap, faded, adhesive letters that announced 'ALISON BURNLEY & Co. BOOKKEEPING' got a muted 'Come in,' followed by a bout of coughing.

The inside was an extension of the faded exterior. Miss Alison Burnley was a very large lady, the kind that wear smocks because their size is not stocked by ladies' clothes shops. She sat behind an old wooden desk that in its prime had a fine green leather top, but that top had been ravaged by time and neglect. The one thing that Miss Burnley was obviously good at, other than bookkeeping, was smoking; a cigarette hung from her lips, an ashtray on the desk overflowed with red lipstick-smeared dog ends, the room had a definite hanging fog of tobacco smoke and the ceiling showed the tell-tale amber tinge of many years of lingering smoke.

'What can I do for you?' asked Burnley, her fat fingers stubbing out the cigarette in the ashtray.

Gheeta looked but couldn't see a fire alarm on the ceiling, which was a bit worrying as there would be no way the rotund bookkeeper would be able to exit from around her desk in a hurry if need be. In fact, Gheeta wondered how on earth a lady of such bulk managed the narrow stairs up from the street.

Palmer held his ID out. 'DCS Palmer, Scotland Yard, and this is DS Singh.'

Burnley nodded. 'I wondered when you'd come along. Jim Riley phoned me with the news earlier, said you'd been there. How's he doing, is he okay? Did he take the news badly? He sounded pretty down.'

Palmer removed his trilby and decided to sit down on one of a pair of chairs that at one stage would have matched the leather desk. It was a toss-up which had the worst wear to the leather, the chairs or the desk, but the main reason for Palmer taking a seat was to get his head out of the smoke cloud that hung like a spider's web in the top half of the room. There was a large window looking out to the street below, but whether it had ever been opened was doubtful judging by the dust on the handle.

'He seems to be coping at present,' answered Palmer. 'But often the real shock of events like this takes a while to hit home.'

'It's ridiculous. Geoff and Linda were quite happy, the business was fine, there's no reason for it, none at all.' She leant back and lit another cigarette, offering the pack to Palmer.

'No, no thanks. You said the business was fine – there wasn't any financial problems, no creditors banging on the door that you know of?'

'No, none. The bank balance went up and down with the seasons as you would expect in a garden centre – down in the winter and then up when spring arrived and the gardeners flocked in. He did have a blip a few months ago but that was sorted.'

'A blip?'

'Yes.' She shrugged. 'I feel like I'm talking out of school. Geoff had an Achilles' heel: gambling. Most of the downs in the business finances were due to his gambling debts and not the seasons, although we never mentioned it to Linda.'

'We?'

'Geoff and I – he made me promise not to tell her. He tried to break the habit but he couldn't.'

'What sort of *blip* was it?' asked Palmer.

'An eighty thousand pounds blip, he did the cardinal sin of all gamblers: lost a bit and instead of writing it off and stopping for a while, he chased it, lost more and then chased that – a sort of never-ending spiral into more and more debt. I must have warned him several times that the bank might put a stop on the account, but he was a typical Mr Micawber, always saying '*something will turn up.*'

'You think that debt could have pushed him into suicide?'

'No, because something did turn up, it was settled. One day in the red, then the next day the account was back into the black. I asked him if he'd got a loan or something as I could claim the interest against tax, or at least some of it, but he said no; said he'd got a partner coming into the business who had settled it as part of the deal, for half the business.'

'Really? Who was this partner?'

'I don't know, he wouldn't say. Said the person wanted to remain anonymous – didn't even want to see the books.'

'Well, if he or she wants to see them now they'll have to come to us, we've got them. Will that impact on your work at the garden centre? Riley said you go in once a week to sort the wages and do the banking.'

'No, no that's all right – Geoff used to sign every cheque in the cheque book when a new one arrived, I've still got quite a few left in the current book so any bills falling due I can pay.' She took a long drag on her cigarette, letting it out slowly. 'What happens now?'

'Well, I've no reason to close the business whilst we investigate the reasons behind the Hanleys' deaths, so my advice would be to carry on as normal. My department will talk to the Hanleys' solicitor and the bank and try to contact this partner. Hopefully whoever it is will carry on the business as usual. Thank you for your time, Mrs Burnley.'

'Miss, it's *Miss* Burnley – not had much luck in the husband stakes.' She laughed and then coughed.

'Well, you never know what might turn up... *Miss* Burnley. If you do think of anything that may have worried Mr Hanley, please let us know.'

Gheeta stepped forward and passed her contact card across the desk to Burnley. 'It's a direct line, no infuriating menu to navigate.'

Burnley laughed as she took the card. 'Oh God, don't you just hate those?'

Palmer smiled, put on his hat and hurried out of the office and down the stairs to fresh air as fast as he could, without jogging his sciatica into action.

They stood on the pavement gulping in fresh air.

'So Sergeant, we have a mysterious benefactor-cum-partner emerging from the shadows. Funny how Jim Riley never mentioned that.'

'Maybe he isn't aware of it guv, but if there's a deposit of eighty grand it will show up in the bank accounts in the file we've got. I can do a trace on the bank code and account number and find out where it came from.'

'Maybe you're right and Riley doesn't know about the partnership deal, but the Hanleys' solicitor will – changing from sole owner to partnership involves legal paperwork. I think Michael Whitley will be our next port of call, may as well do it whilst we are in the area.'

Gheeta checked her laptop. 'Twenty-eight the High Street, can't be far down here.'

'Good.' Palmer walked away.

'Guv.'

He stopped and turned.

Gheeta pointed a finger towards their unmarked squad car parked opposite with the driver reading the paper. 'It's two forty-five, don't you think you should let the driver go and get a sandwich and a drink?'

Palmer looked across the road. 'Yes, yes of course. Time flies, doesn't it? Go and tell him to take a break for half an hour.'

Gheeta did so as Palmer wandered off down the road looking for number twenty-eight. She noted that as usual, no reference to either Gheeta or Palmer getting food and drink had even crossed his mind, but this was usual for Palmer. When a case was running his mind was totally immersed in it; any thoughts of food, drink and time were parked in a small back room somewhere in his brain.

Number twenty-eight Watford High Street was chalk and cheese compared to Alison Burnley's hovel of an office: a full glass-fronted state of the art modern build, with large automatic doors that slid silently open to let Palmer and Gheeta walk through into a spacious foyer where several receptionists sat using keyboards and manning several phone lines. All eyes turned to Gheeta in her uniform.

Palmer presented his ID card to a young man whose badge said he was '*PHILIP. CLIENT SUPPORT*'

'How can we help you, Detective Chief Superintendent?' Philip asked, reading from Palmer's card.

Palmer liked that; full deference, nice touch. He smiled at Philip. 'I wonder if your Michael Whitley could spare us a few minutes?'

'I'll certainly ask his secretary, sir. Might I ask what it is in connection with?'

'The murder of Geoffrey Hanley.'

That shook Philip speechless for a few moments; he wasn't sure what to say to that. He regained his composure. 'One moment please.' He dialled an internal phone and spoke to whoever answered, explaining that Palmer was here and what his business was. There was a short wait before the answer came back. Philip smiled at Palmer and Singh. 'Would you both like to take a seat? Mr Whitley is with a client at present and will be with you as soon as he finishes. Shouldn't be long.' He indicated a row of plush seats in a waiting area.

Palmer and Gheeta sat down. Gheeta took advantage of the free coffee machine. 'Want one, guv?'

'No, I'm fine thank you Sergeant.' Palmer was a coffee man, but only French strength five, percolated for ten minutes; to be offered instant was an insult in his book. He looked at Gheeta's plastic cup as she sat down.

'Don't spill that onto your shoes, it'll take the shine off.'

Gheeta ignored him; it was very welcome, seeing that the last drink she'd had that day was tea with her breakfast at seven in the morning.

It wasn't too long before a call came through to *Philip. Client Support* who came over and asked them to follow him.

'Mr Whitley is free now and will see you.'

He led them through large double doors at the rear of the foyer area and down a wide, plush carpeted corridor with offices off each side. Michael Whitley's office bore his name on the door. Philip knocked before holding the door open for Palmer and Singh to go in.

They were met and greeted by Michael Whitley who stood up from his large modern desk and came round it, hand outstretched.

'Detective Chief Superintendent Palmer, how good to meet you.'

They shook hands and Palmer introduced Gheeta. Michael Whitley was in his forties, obviously fit, and immaculately dressed in solicitor regulation dark blue suit and brown brogues, with a Westminster College tie shouting out his elite credentials for the job.

'Sit down, sit down.' He waved them towards comfortable sofas around the walls and retook his own desk chair. 'Coffee, tea?'

'No, no we are fine, thank you,' said Palmer. 'We won't take up too much of your time Mr Whitley, and thank you for fitting us in at such short notice.'

'Mr Palmer – may I call you Mister?'

'Please do.'

'Mr Palmer, any officer coming into the office and asking to talk about the murder of one of our oldest clients isn't going to be turned away, I can assure you. Geoff Hanley murdered? Tell me more.'

Palmer recounted the story and the basic facts as far as he felt was necessary; he didn't mention poison, just murder.

'So you see Mr Whitley, we are without any suspects at present, although no doubt some will emerge as we dig deeper into the Hanleys' lifestyle. But neither Riley nor the company bookkeeper could give us any information on the new business partner. I was hoping you would have the identity, as being Hanley's solicitor you would have had to be involved with the legalities of the ownership change from sole trader to partnership?'

Whitley looked bewildered. 'I can't help you there Mr Palmer, this is the first I've heard of it. We've not been approached by Mr Hanley to incorporate the company into a partnership. I can't think he'd use anybody else.' He shook his head in disbelief. 'Geoff Hanley was one of our original clients from way back when my father started the business. Dad only retired last year, he will be shocked by this news – they were very good friends, both mad on roses. Many a time Dad would pop over to the Garden Centre at Borehamwood for the quarterly health check on the accounts and come back with a boot full of roses. I never saw him raise an invoice for the visits either.' He gave a sad laugh. 'I don't suppose he'll get his Midnight Glory now.'

'Midnight Glory?' Palmer didn't understand.

'Yes, both bred roses, Dad as an amateur but Geoff was a master at it. Been breeding roses for decades, one of the top breeders in the country was Geoff, and like all of them the final goal is a pure black rose, never been bred. Dad said Geoff was near, but not quite there. You have to jump through so many hoops to get a rose listed as a genuine new type – I don't know much about it, I'm not a gardener like Dad, but apparently whoever gets the Rights Certification for a black rose from the Plant Variety Rights Office or whatever they are called, then that person is a millionaire overnight.'

'A millionaire?' Palmer couldn't believe what he was hearing, nor could Gheeta. A probable reason to murder two people had just appeared.

THURSDAY

Palmer knew the second day of the case would be probably the most important, or one of the most important days. It followed the usual path of every new case: day one you get acquainted with the case, the people involved so far and possible avenues for further investigation; day two you start to put the jigsaw together and start down those avenues of investigation.

With Gheeta's bespoke computer programmes and Claire's skill at shaking out leads with the determination of a dog with a rag, Palmer knew he was in good hands.

His first port of call on the way to the office was the Paddington Secure Evidence Yard where the Transit van was parked. Reg Frome was already at work in it and under it with his forensic team, all in white paper suits, overshoes, hats and gloves. Palmer stood away from them until Frome noticed him and came over.

'Good morning, Justin. Not going to be much help here I'm afraid.'

'No prints?' Palmer was disappointed.

'Some off the driver's cab and steering wheel but nothing in the back. Hardly surprising really when you realise it's a garden centre's van – probably been hosed out many times in the past. We've collected stuff from the drainage hole but it looks like it's mostly plant debris. I'll take the length of hose that was run from the exhaust to the plug hole back to the lab; it's not your everyday garden hose – about three times the diameter, but most likely common in garden centres –

but you never know, we might get a print off it.'

'Okay, there's two people's prints I would like you to ignore, the garden centre manager and the bookkeeper. I don't think they are involved, but their prints will probably show up on things and you can eliminate them. I'll have my Sergeant get the local boys to go round and take their prints and DNA and pass them to you.'

'Yes, that's fine. I'll run them through the national database though. If one turns out to be a serial killer I'll let you know.' Frome smiled.

Palmer couldn't imagine Alison Burnley being able to swat a fly, let alone murder anybody – unless they'd stolen her cigarettes!

'Talking about your Sergeant,' said Frome, 'She gave me a call earlier. She wants to pass some bank papers from this case onto Pete Atkins to have a look at; apparently there's a large payment made to the deceased and she'd like to know who made it. I told her to give him a call.'

Pete Atkins was the forensic accountant attached to Frome's squad. Atkins's previous career was in the city, where he worked for a major bank in the acquisitions and takeover department handling the takeover of companies by other companies, before moving up into the wealth advisory department which basically was charged with finding ways for the rich elite to hide or transfer accumulated wealth that they preferred HMRC not to know about; in layman's language it's called money laundering, in bankers' language it's called wealth advice. Atkins, who came from a normal working class background, was not happy with the banking industries' deference to these elite rich and often major criminal types, and so he left behind the six figure bonuses and champagne lunches and moved into the legal department of the yard's forensic squad under Reg Frome. The poacher became the gamekeeper.

****

Back in the Team Room Gheeta and Claire were delving away into the back grounds of Hanley, Riley and Burnley. Nothing out of the ordinary or causing concern was showing up so far. But Gheeta had some interesting information from another source to pass onto Palmer as he took off his coat and hat and told them that Frome had drawn blanks on the Transit van.

'This rose breeding lark is big business guv,' said Gheeta. 'It's a bit like the music and publishing business. If you can breed a new rose and get a certificate, you get royalties on every one sold. It's policed by BARB – the British Association of Rose Breeders – who are responsible for collecting the royalties on roses that get a certificate. If Hanley was a top breeder like that solicitor said then they should know him, and maybe know others who he was competing with for the black rose, maybe worth a chat with them?'

'Yes, you may be right. I'll give them a call later.'

A knock on the door announced the arrival of Pete Atkins. He still gave the impression of a young city type with his Savile Row suits and Ralph Lauren shirts, topped off with a very handsome face and immaculately styled hair.

'DS Atkins, come in young man.' Palmer liked Atkins. 'Have you found our secret benefactor?'

Atkins sat at a table and opened a file as they gathered round.

'I have found your benefactor sir, and I think it might surprise you.'

'Go on.'

'Well, from the bank statement that DS Singh emailed me I was able to see that the eighty thousand pounds payment came from a Santander Bank account – it's pretty simple to find that out as all account codes relate to certain banks. Now, having got that information I was able to take the account number and work out which branch it was from, and it was a business account – so no branch, as all their business accounts come from a business hub. That's where it gets tricky, as other than hacking into the bank...'

Palmer covered his eyes, hoping beyond hope that Atkins hadn't.

'Don't worry sir, I didn't.'

Palmer breathed a sigh of relief.

'I rang an old mate at the City branch of Santander and he got the information for me. The account belongs to Edward and Janet Bloom, who trade under the name Bloom's Garden Centres with a Watford address. I think that ties in well with this case, doesn't it?'

Gheeta nodded. 'Yes it certainly does. Thanks Peter, that's really helpful.'

Atkins closed the file. 'I'll put it all in an official report and send it through.' He stood to leave. 'One more thing – I think you might find Mr Bloom interesting. I had a quick look on file and it seems we know him already.' He nodded to Palmer and left.

'I'll pull up all we have on Edward and Janet Bloom,' said Claire, returning to her workstation. 'Give me a couple of minutes.'

'Interesting eh, guv?' said Gheeta. 'Looks like one garden centre coming to the rescue of another garden centre, if the money came from the Blooms.'

'Good name for a garden centre, Blooms. They'll get a shock when the news reaches them that Hanley's dead; and if the partnership hadn't been registered the money's gone too.'

'Hang on a minute, I want to check something,' Gheeta said and sat at her keyboard and worked for a minute. 'No, nothing's changed. Company's House still has Hanley's as a sole trader; it's not been changed to a partnership and it's not in review, so there's not a change going through their system at present either.'

'So Blooms haven't a claim on the money they gave Hanley, or on half the actual business?' asked Palmer.

'Well, I'm not a lawyer guv, but it certainly looks that way.'

'That's enough to make you a bit angry, isn't it? Eighty grand down the drain and no legal right to claim it back.' Palmer raised his eyebrows.

'I wouldn't like to be the one who tells them,' Gheeta added.

Claire sat back. 'You might actually like to be the one who tells them, guv. Mr Bloom doesn't seem to be the helpful benefactor he comes across as.'

'Go on.'

Claire read from her screen. 'Edward John Bloom, aged 64. Numerous convictions for petty theft as a young man, seven years in and out of remand centres, finally jailed for seventeen years aged 32 for the armed robbery of a Securicor van in Manchester in 1995; five million taken in the raid and very little recovered. Let out on parole after 12 years, served his parole without any problems and not heard of since.'

'Until now,' Palmer stood and moved to behind Claire and read the screen. 'Keep digging on Mr Bloom, he's just become suspect number one. I think the Blooms' garden centre deserves a visit.'

'Garden centres, guv,' said Gheeta, pointing to the Bloom Garden Centres website she had pulled up on her screen. 'There's three of them, and they look pretty impressive too.'

'I wonder if Mr Bloom is a rose breeder?'

'You're thinking what I'm thinking, guv.'

'Midnight Glory.'

'Yes.'

'I think a call to The British Association of Rose Breeders might pay dividends. What's the number?'

The call to BARB did indeed pay dividends. The secretary was somewhat shaken by the news of Hanley's death; Palmer didn't go into details about the poison, just said that it was an accident and he was trying to find out as much about Hanley as possible because there didn't seem to be any relatives to take control of the business. He put the phone on speaker so Gheeta and Claire could hear.

'No, I don't believe there are any relatives. If there are Geoff never mentioned them,' said the BARB secretary. 'God, what an awful thing to happen – both he and Linda killed in one accident. Awful, he was a lovely chap.'

'And a good rose breeder so we are told,' said Palmer.

'Oh yes indeed, one of the top few. We have many named roses that belong to him. Quite a few breeders achieve double figures, and high double figures at that; Geoff was one of those. It's a long process to breed a new rose Chief Superintendent, eight to ten years from the initial crossing of pollen from selected plants, and then no guarantee of success. It has to be pretty nigh perfect to pass the National Institute of Agricultural Botany trials and tests and go on to the PVRO for intellectual property rights to be given.'

'I'm told Mr Hanley was determined to breed the first black rose.'

The secretary laughed. 'The Holy Grail of rose breeders everywhere. Yes, and he was damn near to doing it too. He sent an example to the NIAB two years ago and it was bloody close, but just not quite jet black. They were expecting another one next year from him – might well have cracked it by then.'

'Instant fame and fortune then?'

'Well, not instant, no. If the trials proved good and he got a certificate then Geoff would take cuttings and bud wood – that's small pieces of stem with a bud on – and grow them on and then repeat the process for a couple of years himself, and we would license growers to commercially grow on and multiply the stock until there was enough to go to market. The market for a black rose would be enormous; tens of thousands of plants would be sold through garden centres and mail order, and that's just the UK. But don't be deceived, as I said before it's a long haul – can be upwards of eight years to breed a rose good enough to trial.'

'I don't know whether you can answer this, but was Mr Hanley's income from rose breeding substantial?'

'Substantial? No. The market fluctuates a lot; one season everybody wants yellow and the next everybody wants red. Geoff's stable is a good one and would give him and Linda a couple of decent holidays every year, but you couldn't live on it unless you were very frugal.'

'I bet the chap who bred Peace lives on the royalties from that one.' Palmer felt quite proud that he'd remembered the name of at least one rose in Mrs P.'s garden.

'I'm afraid he doesn't. That entered commerce in 1945, long before Plant Breeders Rights were in existence; and even now rose royalties like other plant royalties only last twenty-five years, and then it's a free-for-all.'

'Are there many rose breeders then?'

'Not many individuals, it's more of a hobby than a good business proposition. Don't forget they are up against the professional business growers with massive greenhouses and hundreds of thousands of seedlings growing away; they can do very well on growing existing roses for the trade.'

'Ever heard of a grower called Bloom, Edward Bloom?'

There was a telltale silence on the line for moment.

'Oh yes, we've heard of Edward Bloom. I wish we had never heard of him. Why do you ask?'

'Well, and I must ask for you to keep this confidential, it seems that Mr Bloom may have made a partnership offer to Mr Hanley.'

'Geoff wouldn't touch him with a bargepole. Let me tell you about Edward Bloom. He first came to our notice some years ago when he worked for a lovely lady called Angela Robinson, who had a garden centre in Watford and another in Stanmore – two good centres too, and she bred roses as well. Bloom was an ex-convict who had met Angela when she visited the open prison at Pentonville to run a garden club and an allotment for the inmates. They hit it off, and when Bloom was released he began to work for her; a year later they married, and I have to say that everybody I know who met Bloom took an instant dislike to him and wondered what on earth had possessed Angela to marry him. Within a year she was dead, accident with a chain saw, and Bloom inherited the centres and moved in a young lady thirty years his junior who had recently graduated from the Pershore Agricultural College as his new wife and business partner. I have no need to tell you, Chief Superintendent, of the rumours that circulated within the business.'

'I can imagine.'

'It gets better, or maybe I should say worse. Angela had always bred roses and had quite a few licensed through us. Well after her death new ones were still coming into us for trials from the Blooms on a regular basis – nothing wrong in that, except after about three years we noticed a distinct similarity between the ones Blooms was putting in and those from other breeders. It's a close-knit community Chief Superintendent, very close-knit, and a lot of peer group support. We made a few discreet enquiries and found that the Blooms were often visiting other breeders on the pretext of asking for help with something to do with garden centres, or just simply turning up unannounced – *we were just passing.* Have you met Mrs Bloom, Chief Superintendent ?'

'No, not yet.'

'Well, when you do you'll understand why a late middle-aged gardener might well have his attention riveted on her – so much so that he might not notice a new bud wood growth or seedling disappear from the row on his bench into Mr Bloom's rucksack that he always carried over his shoulder. Anyway, to cut a long story short a trap was laid and sprung and the Blooms were thrown out of the Association, and I hope never to see them again. So you see, no way would Geoff have entertained a business partnership with them.'

Claire pushed a written note in front of Palmer. *They have 3 centres, not 2.*

'Where did the Blooms' third garden centre come from? Did they expand?'

'Yes, they bought Charlie Hilton's garden centre in Barnet. Charlie was getting on a bit – had a dicky heart, no family and looking to retire, so it suited him, all legal and above board as far as I know.'

You've been very helpful sir, very helpful indeed. Thank you for your time and once again I'd ask you to keep our conversation confidential if you would.'

'Of course, anything else I can help with just give me a call.'

Palmer ended the call. 'Well, the Blooms certainly have my attention now. Do they have an office?'

Claire scrolled her screen. 'The main garden centre is at Stanmore which has the main phone line.'

'Give it a call, see if we can get to see them in the morning'

****

'What did you do? What the hell have you done?'

Jim Riley let Edward and Janet Bloom into his bedsit. They had been waiting in their car outside for him to get home from work. Edward was mid-sixties, with greying hair and a paunch, wearing a dark grey suit and looking anything but a gardener. Janet, early thirties, slim and blonde (from a bottle) was in a designer trouser suit and ankle boots; she looked fit and business-like.

'Calm down Jim, it's all under control.' Edward motioned him to sit.

'Calm down? Under control? I've had the police round asking questions, they said the Hanleys had committed suicide in the back of the van, found in a motorway car park.' He sat on the edge of the bed as the Blooms took the two chairs beside his small table. 'You killed them, didn't you? You murdered them for the black rose!'

There was no answer.

'You did, you killed them! Christ, what's going on? The police have kept the van, said the exhaust was piped inside and killed them.'

'They robbed us, Jim.' Janet Bloom spoke softly. 'They broke their promise of a partnership.'

'What? What do you mean? How could they rob you?'

'They took the eighty grand that bailed them out of debt and kept the bailiffs away on the promise of a partnership, and then decided they didn't want a partnership.'

'So what, take the money back and that's it, the end?'

'The money was gone, Jim – paid off the debts, all gone. We offered to let them pay it back bit by bit, but Geoff wouldn't. He laughed at us – he said he knew all along you'd been giving us some of his bud wood and seeds. He was going to press charges against us, and you.'

'What did you do, tie them up and run the exhaust until they were dead?'

'I poisoned them,' said Janet.

'WHAT?'

'It was a spur of the moment thing, it wasn't planned. They sat in our kitchen, Jim, and basically laughed at us – said we wouldn't get any of the money back, wouldn't get a partnership, and would probably get a prison sentence for stealing the rose, and so would you. They laughed at us. I was so angry I could have strangled the gloating pair of them, I was making tea at the time and the temptation was too great – I slipped a spoonful in their cups. It's tasteless.'

'What poison?'

'Aconite, I'd had it in the cupboard for ages, made it to get rid of a few rats in the greenhouses ages ago.'

Jim sank his head into his hands. 'Oh for God's sake. They know, the police know.'

'No they don't, the police think it was suicide,' Edward Bloom said forcibly. 'And that's all there is to it. Just stay calm and this will all calm down. We will be able to prove we paid the money to Hanley, and then everything will get back to normal and we will have the centre.'

'Did you hear me?' Jim shouted at Bloom. 'I said the police fucking know! The Sergeant asked me if we sold Aconites – why would she ask that, eh? They know!'

They sat in silence for a few moments before Janet spoke

'Even if the police know they died from poison, it's alright. It just means the Hanleys took aconite before turning on the exhaust; after all they were garden experts, they would know it's a poison and so they used it to make sure of the suicide. The police can't tie it to us.'

'That damn black rose, eh? You have to have it, don't you? And now you've murdered two people to get it.' Jim stared coldly at Edward. 'I was so stupid, wasn't I? You played me all along. When Janet came into the centre I thought it was just coincidence – coincidence that the girl I loved at college had turned up again; coincidence that she spilled her heart out to me about a loveless marriage with you. It was just a sham, a ploy, wasn't it? A ploy to get to me and the black rose.'

Edward Bloom gave a sarcastic laugh and pointed to the bed Jim was sitting on. 'You didn't mind that when you were shagging her on that cheap bed, did you?

'He knows?' Riley looked at Janet.

Bloom laughed louder. 'Knew? Of course I knew, I planned it you fool! You think a girl as attractive as Janet would go for you without a good reason? I want that rose and I'll have that rose. You get our van over to Hanley's in the morning, load the plants – the bud wood and seedlings of the black rose – and get them over to Watford. That black rose is going to be unveiled at the Chelsea Flower Show next Monday for the press and the royal visit, and it will be there under the Bloom name.'

'It won't – I'm going to the police in the morning. I'm not getting involved in murder, I'll take whatever I get for theft of Hanley's roses, but not murder. No.'

Edward Bloom's mood got nasty. He leant forward face-to-face with Jim and jabbed a finger into his chest. 'You do that Riley, and you'd better get police protection for yourself, understand me? You just do as I say, you stick to your story – you're not involved, you don't even know about the partnership. You didn't tell the police you knew, did you?'

'No.'

'Good, then keep it that way and everything will work out fine. Here.' He took a key out of his pocket. 'This is for the door to the staff entrance at the Watford Centre. Put everything in the rose house.'

****

'What do you think you are doing?'

Mrs P. and Daisy the dog stood in Palmer's porch at his house in Dulwich Village, looking at him stumbling about in her front garden rose bed. 'Get your size elevens out of there before you do some damage.'

Palmer had got home and parked his CRV on the drive when the thought had struck him: *perhaps, just perhaps?* He looked over to the porch.

'I'm looking for a black one.'

'A black what?'

'Rose, a black rose.'

'Don't be stupid, you've got more chance of finding Shergar in there than a black rose.

Your dinner's on the table – lasagne with burnt cheese topping.'

The thought of one of his favourite dishes immediately put paid to the rose bed search and he carefully made his way out of it, knowing that one broken stem would bring down fire and brimstone if Mrs P. found it.

He left his shoes in the porch in case they were dirty, padded his way down the hall, put his coat and hat on the hallstand, rescued his slippers from Daisy's jaw and went into the kitchen.

'Smells nice.'

Mrs P. carried on eating hers. 'I take it the foray into the rose bed has something to do with a case at work?'

Palmer gave her a brief outline of the case between mouthfuls of lasagne.

'So you think this Bloom character is after the black rose, which you don't even know exists?' Mrs P. had a habit of throwing water on the fire.

'Yes, it will exist, mark my words. Everything points towards its existence, otherwise why would two people be dead?'

'Did you enjoy that lasagne?

'Yes, lovely.'

'It was vegetarian.'

'Tasted awful.'

The ongoing battle in the Palmers' kitchen was Mrs P.'s attempts to get Palmer to eat less meat and onto a more healthy diet, both for his own sake and the planet's.

'I'll get a Big Mac later when I take Daisy out.'

'You'll do no such thing. She's on a diet, the vet said she should lose a kilo.'

'She's fine, she gets taken out for walks twice a day.'

'Once a day, with me in the morning – your so-called '*dog walk*' in the evening is up the road to Dulwich Park and back again.'

'Yes, so?'

'When you've done the one hundred metres to the park gate Justin, the idea is to go inside and walk round the park, not turn round and come home and then give her a large fatty treat for being a good girl. Anyway, talking about roses, Benji is going to make his front garden into a rose garden like ours.'

'He only had it paved over last year.'

Benji, full name Benjamin Courtney-Smith, was Palmer's next-door neighbour and nemesis. A retired advertising executive in his early sixties, spray on tan, ponytail, designer clothes and, in Palmer's estimation, of questionable sexual orientation, judging by the mincing walk and habit of waving a floppy hand about when talking. Too much money and too much time on his hands was Palmer's usual anti-Benji mantra; three or four continental cruises or holidays a year, a new motor every year, and Palmer reckoned a new nip and tuck every year too. But Benji was a great favourite with most of the ladies in the area, especially Mrs P. and her gardening club and WI, and this rankled a bit with Palmer who was their favourite until Benji moved in and knocked him off that plinth. Then, to cap it all, he ran for the local council elections and got voted in; he was soon elevated to Chairperson and became everybody's favourite by reinstating pensioner free bus passes and pool passes for the over 50's. He then had topped it off by twisting arms at the county level to secure funding to re-open the library that the previous council had closed due to financial cuts. But he was also prone to accidents, usually involving Palmer's property.

'He's got a mini-digger coming in the morning to take up the paving and some topsoil being delivered later on.'

'What about the roses themselves?'

'He wants me to go with him to a garden centre and choose some.'

'Don't go to Bloom's.'

'I'm not going all that way. We'll go local, there's a good one in Norwood. He only wants roses without thorns – he's allergic to pricks.'

'You could have fooled me.'

FRIDAY

'It's all very interesting sir,' said Claire, turning from her computer to Palmer who was reading the report from Pete Atkins. Gheeta was sticking photos of the deceased on the big white progress board at the far end of the room and drawing felt tip arrows to the names of the other people in the case: Riley, Burnley, the Blooms. Bit by bit those lines would grow into a pattern as the case progressed and a tie between the people shown became apparent; they always did.

Palmer raised his head from the report. 'What's all very interesting?'

'Breeding roses. It's a bit like sex.'

'How's your memory, guv?' Gheeta said from the end of the room.

'Very funny, Sergeant. Carry on, Claire.'

Claire turned back to her screen and read from it. 'Well, first you select the two roses you want to cross and take the petals off the flower of the mother plant, leaving the green outer petals which are called anthers, and then remove all the inside except for the stigma – that's the central bit. After a while that will go sticky, which means it's ready for the father's pollen from the other plant. Using a soft paintbrush you put the pollen from that one onto the stigma, then put a small paper bag over the flower and leave it for a few days for the pollination to take place. Then you grow it on until the rose hip develops, which is the seed pod, and when that's ripe you take the seeds out and leave them in a fridge to simulate winter conditions until the next

January. Then plant them and cross your fingers.'

'And commercial growers do this thousands of times to get one good one?'

'They do.'

'And obviously nobody's hit on a black one yet.'

'Which is why it would be worth so much,' said Gheeta, joining them.

'And worth stealing,' said Palmer. 'Our chat with the Blooms is going to be an interesting one.'

Gheeta walked back from the board and gave Palmer an enquiring look. 'You think Hanley had bred one, don't you guv? You think the black rose is what this is all about, don't you?'

'I do.' He turned to Claire. 'Has the CCTV recordings from the motorway services come through yet?'

'Not yet, sir. They quoted the Data Protection Act so I've had our legal department issue an exemption notice – should be here soon.'

****

Palmer had asked DS Singh to be in normal clothes for the visit to the Blooms; he wanted to take a quiet look around before announcing his arrival.

The Bloom's Stanmore centre was obviously the jewel in the crown. It had five large greenhouses, a restaurant, child's play area, aquarium and gift shop.

'Impressive, eh?' Palmer said to Gheeta as they got out of his car and walked towards the busy entrance. Plain squad cars have a habit of standing out amongst others, so he had opted to drive to Stanmore in his own.

'Very impressive, guv. You know I was thinking about Edward Bloom's seventeen-year stretch for the Manchester robbery – hardly any of the five million was traced and it was before the days of the Proceeds of Crime Act, so I suppose it was just written off by the insurance company?'

'Very probably, why?'

'Well, three very busy garden centres would be a good way of laundering quite substantial amounts of cash if it was still around, wouldn't they guv.'

'They would.' He thought for a moment. 'Have that Atkins chap take a look at the posted accounts of Blooms since he inherited it, and do a quick comparison with the years before and after. I take it HMRC would have them archived somewhere?'

'They have guv, and they show an increase of a hundred and twenty thousand on the first year of his ownership, rising to an increase of just on three hundred thousand pounds in the last accounts.'

Palmer stopped walking, as did Singh. His cold stare met her pair of innocent eyes. Palmer had pulled DS Singh out of the Yard's Cyber Crime and IT Unit after she had upgraded his office HOLMES programme in an hour after it had '*gone down*', a job that the outside contractors usually took two days to do and then probably only after waiting a week for a visit. Palmer had for some time realised the value of computers and their various programmes in the pursuit of criminals, and felt that having to use the overworked in-house unit at the Yard and the wait that entailed had to be overcome. What better way to overcome it than to prise one of their top programmers away and into his squad? Gheeta didn't need asking twice.

Palmer's immediate boss, AC Bateman was not keen on asking for her transfer, as he didn't want to upset the AC whose command the Cyber Unit came under; Bateman didn't want to upset anybody in his quest to reach the post of Commissioner and crept around everybody. Not to be beaten, Palmer had a quiet word with the chairman of the House of Commons Home Affairs Select Committee, an old school MP who, like Palmer, didn't hold much truck with PC and some human rights issues; he in turn had a word with the

Commissioner, and Gheeta was transferred to Palmer's Serial Murder Squad within seven days. AC Bateman then did a quick about-turn and made a big thing of welcoming her, and made out that his input had clinched the transfer; but everybody knew that wasn't so.

The unwritten law between Gheeta and Palmer was that she had *carte blanche* to install whatever programmes she thought might be useful, but he didn't want to know about the ones she hacked from other law enforcement agencies worldwide, or any other below-the-line IT and cyber activities she downloaded from the dark web and used in the pursuit of criminals.

Palmer shook his head in recognition that he knew how Gheeta had come by the information on Bloom's accounts. 'Okay, but get Atkins to do it as well, legally – just in case we need to use it in evidence, got to be within the law.'

They wandered through the wide entrance into the first greenhouse. Gheeta picked up a steel basket from the pile. 'How much can I spend, guv?'

'You live in a fifth-floor apartment in the Barbican, Sergeant. You haven't got a garden.'

'I could do with some house plants to brighten the place up.'

'You're not there to water them, they'd die.'

'Seeing that we are out of uniform guv, does that mean that I'm off duty at the moment?'

'No, why?'

'Because if I was off duty at present I'd be classed as a civilian and I'd call you a mean old bastard.'

Palmer laughed, 'Water off a duck's back, Sergeant. Mrs P. calls me that all the time, and worse.'

'She'd have a ball in here wouldn't she, guv?'

'She would indeed. She's off to a local garden centre today with our neighbour – he's starting a rose garden and they're choosing the plants.'

Gheeta pointed to a sign board standing at the back of the greenhouse beside the exit into a courtyard. An arrow pointed through with ROSES under it. 'That might be interesting, guv.'

They walked through into the courtyard which was full of large pots of shrubs and fruit bushes. Halfway through Gheeta grabbed Palmer's arm and stopped him.

'Do you see what I see, guv?'

He had – it was a coiled hose for use in watering the plants, not the normal domestic garden hose but exactly like the one in the Hanley van that Frome had left them a photo of. Gheeta took out her mobile phone and made as though taking photos of the bushes, but zooming in on the hose – *click, click*.

'Can I help you?' a female voice asked. 'Having trouble making your mind up?'

They turned round as a young Bloom's worker approached them with a big smile on her face. 'There's so many fruit varieties it's difficult to choose. Which type are you after?'

Gheeta took the lead. 'Blackcurrants. My grandfather here is thinking of starting a fruit patch and he's keen on blackcurrants.'

The assistant gave Palmer a smile. 'Good choice sir, plenty of vitamin C in blackcurrants. What type of soil do you have?'

'Sort of dark grey,' said Palmer before he could stop himself.

The assistant laughed and Gheeta managed a false one too.

'Do you live locally, sir?'

'Yes.' Gheeta though it best if she took over the conversation. 'Just half a mile away.'

'Okay, then you'll have a good loam soil and we recommend the variety Ben Connan.' The assistant pointed to a bush dripping with blackcurrants ready to pick. 'It's a good large currant, as you can see, and very sweet – likes a loam soil and best kept a little damp, which is not hard with the English weather.'

'Ben Connan,' repeated Gheeta. 'Right, thank you for that. Now we are going to have a look at the roses.'

'You're welcome, just carry on through the next greenhouse and the rose house is on the right. Anything else we can help you with just ask one of the assistants.'

'We will, thank you.'

The assistant wandered off.

Palmer stood and looked Gheeta in the eyes, impassive.

'What?'

'Father I could take, but grandfather? You cheeky sod.'

Gheeta smiled and shrugged. They made their way to the rose house; it was enormous – at least fifty metres long and twenty wide – with paths running between benches packed with roses of all sizes, types and colours, as well as being packed with buyers.

They stood at the entrance taking it all in.

'Mr Palmer.' A voice shouted his name from behind them where Janet Bloom was hurrying through the greenhouse towards them. She was wearing a green trouser suit with Bloom's logo across the chest, green suede ankle boots and green cap hiding her blonde locks. Gheeta noted that the top of the suit was unbuttoned to reveal a certain amount of cleavage. She nudged Palmer.

'Down boy.'

Palmer smiled. 'No chance – not unless she makes a pretty mean steak and kidney pie.'

'I thought it must be you,' gushed Janet Bloom as she reached them, flapping her false eyelashes at Palmer so much Gheeta thought she felt a draft. 'We spoke to Jim Riley last night, and he said you'd been round and gave us a description. I'm Janet Bloom.'

Palmer took the outstretched hand and introduced Gheeta as DS Singh.

'What an awful state of affairs with Geoff and Linda. We never saw that coming at all, they seemed so happy – anyway, I'm forgetting my manners. Do come over to the office, Edward's over there.' She noticed the empty basket Gheeta was carrying. 'We won't get very rich with you two as customers, will we?' she laughed. 'Let me take that.'

She took the basket and slid it under a bench.

The office was through a keypad-protected door marked 'STAFF ONLY'. Inside was the opposite to Jim Riley's office: modern office furniture, two computer workstations, and two water coolers dispensing Malvern or Buxton spring water depending on your choice, both regularly filled with Stanmore tap water – Janet Bloom was very frugal with the company's money. Edward Bloom stood up from his chair behind the wide metal desk and was introduced.

'Edward, this is Detective Chief Superintendent Palmer and Detective Sergeant Singh. They are investigating Geoff and Linda's suicide.' She opened her hand towards Edward as he came round the desk. 'My husband, Edward.'

They shook hands coldly. Palmer was of course fully aware of Edward Bloom's criminal past, and Edward Bloom fully aware that Palmer would be.

'Do sit down.' He pointed them towards a pair of contemporary design Danish sofas that matched the desk; if nothing else Janet Bloom had some taste. She took a seat on a matching chair as Edward went back to his desk. 'Can I order you tea or coffee?'

Palmer removed his trilby and shook his head. 'Thank you, no. We've a lot to get through today so trying to keep toilet breaks to a minimum.'

They all laughed.

'I can't understand why this awful suicide is interesting the police so much,' said Janet. 'I know it's a terrible thing to happen but it's not a crime, is it?'

Funny way of putting it, thought Gheeta.

'And I doubt it will be the last, Mrs Bloom,' said Palmer, flashing her his killer smile. 'Trouble is it gets a bit involved when there's two of them in strange circumstances.'

'Strange circumstances?' Edward showed interest.

'Very strange circumstances, sir. For instance why would they drive to a motorway service station to do it, easier to run the exhaust into the van in their own garage, or at their garden centre after work? Why go to a motorway service station? Very strange.'

Janet Bloom changed the subject. 'You do know that we have a financial interest in the Hanley Garden centre Mr Palmer, don't you?'

'I wasn't aware, no.' Palmer laid the trap.

'Yes, we put a considerable amount of money into it on a partnership basis. The Hanleys were old friends of ours and had hit a bad patch; basically we helped them out and they gratefully offered a partnership.'

'Really? How did you know they had, as you put it, *'hit a bad patch'*?'

The silence was deafening.

Edward broke it. 'Our bookkeeper told us. She does the Hanley books as well as ours and was quite worried.

'Not very professional of her was it, discussing one client's business with another client?'

Janet Bloom gave a false laugh. 'Well, she knew we were great friends and she was very worried for Geoff and Linda.'

'So that would be Alison Burnley then?'

'Yes, she's been with us from the start.'

'Before the start surely? She was bookkeeper to Angela Robinson, wasn't she?'

'Yes, yes I believe she was.' Edward Bloom shifted uncomfortably in his chair and was looking at his wife as he answered. Palmer's knowledge had surprised him.

'Funny that. We had a chat with Miss Burnley yesterday and she told us Hanley's problems stemmed from his gambling debts. Did she tell you that?'

'No, no, just that he was in financial trouble. Quite deep financial trouble.'

'Another funny thing is that Miss Burnley said she had no idea who had put the money in to clear the debt. That lady seems to have a very selective memory, doesn't she? I wonder why.'

Silence.

'Are you still breeding roses, Mr Bloom?'

Edward Bloom was getting visibly uncomfortable. 'No, no I don't do any breeding, got enough on our plate without adding to it.' He gave a false laugh.

'BARB told us you used to, before you had a falling out with them. Geoff Hanley bred roses – very successfully too. He was apparently well on the way to the Holy Grail.'

Silence.

'Do you know what the Holy Grail of rose breeding is, Mr Bloom? I'm sure you do.'

'Yes of course, the black rose. Everybody knows that,' smirked Edward Bloom.

'Apparently Geoff Hanley was very near to breeding one. So if he was well on his way to fame and fortune with a black rose that would pay off his debt, why suddenly decide to drive to a Motorway service station, murder his wife and commit suicide?'

'Murder his wife?' Janet Bloom didn't understand.

'Well I don't suppose she leaped at the idea of a suicide pact with her husband, would you?' Palmer stood up. 'Well, we must be off – thank you for seeing us. Just one thing I think you might want to check out – according to the Hanleys' solicitor and the

HMRC files, the Hanley Garden Centre at the time of his death was a sole trader not a partnership – no changes to its constitution have been filed – so maybe you ought to chase that up, because there doesn't seem to be any other directors or living relatives who might register an interest; and in that situation the business will be put in the hands of solicitors to sell and any proceeds handed over to the Treasury. Well, nice to meet you both, but we must be going – things to do, people to see.'

Gheeta closed her laptop which had recorded the conversation and filmed it and followed him out. It wouldn't be acceptable in a court of law as she hadn't asked permission to record or film, and the Blooms hadn't been given an opportunity to have a lawyer present, but it worked as a good aide-memoire should they need it.

'Oh, one thing more,' she said as they all went back into the main glasshouse. 'Do you stock any aconites?'

Both Blooms answered together. 'No', 'It's poisonous', 'No never have.'

****

Back in Palmer's car he gave Gheeta a sly smile and raised his eyebrows. 'Well, how interesting was that?'

'Very interesting guv – very, very interesting.'

'I think we are on the right track, don't you?'

'Definitely, and I should think the phone line between the Blooms and Miss Burnley is red hot by now! I wonder why she didn't mention the Blooms were the providers of money to Hanley? She obviously knew.'

'Which beggars the question is Burnley straight or in cahoots with the Blooms? We need to keep an eye on her. Right, let's take a look at the Hanleys' house – I take it the local boys have taped it off?'

'They have – basic report was nothing out of place. They went in to see if they could find a record of any family relatives, but no joy.'

****

The Hanleys' Borehamwood home was a Victorian semi in a quiet leafy backstreet. The uniformed constable at the gate reported no activity except from nosy locals; Palmer couldn't see the point of keeping him there or of keeping the crime scene tape across the driveway, as it just increased the chance of a nosy local journalist starting to ask questions, and Palmer wasn't ready for any of that just yet. Reg Frome's forensics team had been in and no poison had been found, or indeed anything out of the ordinary at all.

They stood at the front door.

'We should have picked the keys up from the local station on the way here, guv. I didn't think, sorry.'

'Not a problem, Sergeant.' Palmer pulled out a set of lock picks from his coat pocket; years dealing with criminals of all kinds had taught Palmer a few skills that were not on the Hendon graduates' curriculum. DS Singh had seen him use the picks several times in the past and positioned herself behind him, cutting out any view from the street of what was going on.

It only took a few twists and the door was open.

'Well, if you ever fancy a change of career, guv?'

'Probably make more money,' Palmer smiled as they walked into the hall. It was well kept, tidy – a few letters on a half oval side table, nothing out of the ordinary. The dark frost of graphite on the surfaces and painted door jambs showed Frome's fingerprint team had been through.

Palmer checked the ground floor whilst Gheeta had a look through the two bedrooms, spare room and bathroom upstairs; everything was in place, no disturbance anywhere to indicate a fight or anything similar had taken place. The kitchen had a door out to the garden which they could see from the lounge was, as you would expect, immaculate. The flower beds threw out waves of colour along their borders and the lawn was fit for a bowls tournament.

'I hope somebody keeps on top of that, seems a shame if it's let off the lead,' Palmer commented.

'You could get Mrs P. and her Garden Club to come round and keep an eye on it guv,' Gheeta said.

'I'm not even going to mention it to her, or she would. Once all this caper is sorted out and put to bed somebody is going to be able to buy a very nice home here.'

A noise at the front door sent the pair of them into silent mode. Gheeta tiptoed to the lounge door and removing her peaked hat peeped round just as an envelope was dropped through the letterbox and a figure retreated from the door. She hurried into the front room just in time to see Janet Bloom get into a car alongside her husband and drive off.

'Now I wonder what we have here then?' Palmer was turning the envelope over in his hand as she joined him in the hall.

'Something from the Blooms, guv – that was Janet Bloom who popped it through the letterbox and Edward was waiting in the car at the end of the drive.'

'What are they playing at then? You'd hardly send a letter to somebody you know is deceased, would you?'

'I wouldn't guv, and you wouldn't, but the Blooms just have.'

'Let's have a look see then.' Palmer ripped open the envelope, took out a folded letter inside and opened it. He read it silently before passing it to Gheeta.

'Seems our earlier chat with the Blooms has got them worried about their partnership with Hanley.'

Gheeta finished reading. 'Or should we say their non-partnership with Hanley.'

The letter read;

My dear Geoff, It is now a few weeks since you agreed to put the Hanley's Garden Centre into a partnership with Bloom's. You have had the eighty thousand pounds we agreed on for that half share and I am a bit worried that my solicitor has not heard anything from your solicitor. Would you please move things along so we can complete our agreed deal asap. Yours, Edward Bloom.

'See the date.' Palmer pointed to the date at the top of the letter.

'A week ago today,' said Gheeta. 'What are the Blooms playing at?'

'They're trying to manufacture evidence that they were owners of half the Hanley's Garden Centre before the Hanleys died; if they legally were then in law they'd have first option to buy the other half once things settle down.'

'But legally they weren't half owners, guv – nothing had been altered or was in the process of being altered at Companies House. This stupid letter won't change that – and in any case, us witnessing it being delivered today could get them put on a charge of attempted fraud. I'd like that.'

'Yes it could, but I don't want them on attempted fraud – I want them on a murder charge, so this letter is going to disappear. It never existed, did it?'

'What never existed, guv?'

'The letter.'

'What letter?'

Palmer put the letter into his pocket and they left the house.

****

Janet Bloom broke the silence in their car.

'Where are we going now?'

'Burnley's, I want to have a good chat with her and put her right. Stupid woman, fancy saying she wasn't aware we were the people giving Hanley the money? Palmer knows now that she's our bookkeeper as well as Hanley's, because we told him that she told us Hanley had debts. If he asks her again she'll have to say she made a mistake and forgot – memory lapse brought on by shock at the Hanleys' deaths.'

'He suspects we did it as well, you know that don't you? He bloody well suspects us, you could tell from his attitude – and then that sergeant asking if we stock aconites, Jim said she asked him the same question. They know about the poison and they suspect us.'

'There's a big difference between suspecting and proving. They can't prove we had anything to do with it. Our story is strong – we were going into partnership with Hanley, so why would we murder him? Everything was ticking along nicely until the bastard changed his mind. Eighty grand Janet, he stole that eighty grand.'

'You're forgetting where that eighty grand came from.'

Edward Bloom laughed. 'Yes, that had slipped my mind. You have to admit, that was a peach of a plan.'

'Didn't work out though, did it?'

'No, and I don't know why. Do you think Hanley cottoned onto it?'

'No, I think he cottoned onto you and Riley stealing his black rose.'

'Yes, and I mean to keep it. That little treasure is worth a great deal more than eighty grand – you know that and I know that. Get it to market and I'll show those stuck up bastards at BARB. They'll lose thousands of pounds by not collecting on it; they'll be round on their hands and knees asking for the rights management, just you wait and see – and the garden centres and mail order boys will be falling over themselves to stock it in the thousands. I'm not sacrificing that. Burnley won't step out of line, she knows I've got enough on her to send her down for a long time.'

'So why are we going to hers?'

'I want her to have a word with Riley. I'll tell her what to say.'

'Don't forget it's Chelsea on Monday, royal visit and press preview – don't you upset the apple cart before then. I want that black rose as the centre of our display.'

****

Back in the Team Room Claire had some news for Palmer and Gheeta when they walked in.

'Two things of interest: first, the Hanleys' solicitor Mr Whitley rang. He's had a letter from the Blooms' solicitor saying he understands the Hanleys have been paid eighty thousand pounds by his clients in return for a partnership in the garden centre business and when will the paperwork be ready; Whitley has replied that he knows nothing of any partnership deal and had no instruction to effect one before Mr Hanley passed away.'

'That's good.' Palmer was pleased. 'If Bloom's solicitors know their stuff they'll know that without signed papers by Hanley there just isn't any deal. Looks like the Blooms are trying every avenue they can to get Hanley's centre.'

'And the second thing is of more interest I think, sir.' She switched on the large plasma screen on the wall above the bank of Gheeta's computer servers. 'The motorway services CCTV has arrived at last.'

The screen burst into life, showing the lorry park with the numerical LED clock in the corner of the screen showing nine forty-three. The Hanleys' Transit drove into view and backed into a space between two lorries at the back of the area; the area was lit by basic streetlamps that didn't exactly flood the area with light. The picture was very grainy, but a figure could be seen exiting the driver's door and disappearing to the rear of the Transit.

'I think this is when whoever that figure is fixed up the exhaust pipe to the hose,' said Claire.

A time of three minutes elapsed and the corner LED showed nine forty-six as the figure emerged and made off towards the main cafe building and out of CCTV range.

'It's not a lot to go on,' Claire explained. 'But from the counter clock in the corner of the screen we can see the person went into the building at approximately nine forty-six. So, what he or she would need now is a means of leaving the services. They can either leave by this northbound side of the services onto the M25 and travel north or cross the motorway by the services bridge to the south side and travel south. Both sides have a National Express coach service that calls every hour; I checked the internal coach CCTV but nobody who got onto or left those coaches fits the Blooms' description.

'So that leaves the possibility that our Transit driver drove from the services or was driven from them. With the Blooms being suspects *numero uno*, I contacted the DVLA and asked for a list of all vehicles registered to them individually or Bloom's Garden Centres. There are four in total, so I thought going south from the services back towards the motorway exits for the Stanmore and Watford area would be the best bet, and had the Welcome Break CCTV of the south side exit to the motorway onscreen and looked for any of those four vehicles leaving after ten o'clock – that's giving whoever left the Transit about ten minutes to get over the bridge, find the getaway vehicle and drive off. I just prayed they didn't stop for a meal or I'd probably still be looking at number plates now.'

'Is that what you did?' Palmer was amazed at Claire's dexterity.

'Yep, I stopped the CCTV at every vehicle exiting the south side and pulled up the number plate on the enlarger. Fifth car out – bingo! Kia Creed Estate registered to Janet Bloom. We've only got the back view but there are definitely two people in it, driver and passenger.' She sat back. 'I put an ANPR check through on it and guess what?'

'What?' Palmer asked.

'Janet Bloom reported it stolen that afternoon. The police recovered it burnt out on an industrial estate in Watford the following morning.'

'Crafty pair aren't they, eh?' Palmer knew this was an old ploy, usually used by thieves who stole a car to use in a burglary and then torched it to remove all evidence that they were ever in it.

'Well not really, guv,' Gheeta had doubts. 'I mean we've got the car at the services, and the timeframe is right from all angles.'

'Yes it is, but it's all circumstantial – strong circumstantial, I'll give you that, and something we can use. Well done Claire, bloody good work – well done.'

Claire and Gheeta looked at each other in surprise. Praise from Palmer? Unheard of.

****

Palmer was in a good mood as he turned off the road into his short herringbone patterned brick drive at home. Things were coming along nicely in the case, the Blooms were in panic mode, and the evidence, although circumstantial so far, was mounting up. Yes, it had been a good day.

The good day came to a sudden halt as he hit the brakes to avoid running into a mini-digger lying on its side across his herringbone brick drive, part of which now resembled a builder's demolition tip. His eyes followed the deep scrape in the earth back through Mrs P.'s rose garden and through a large hole ripped in the laurel hedge between the Palmer's and Benji's front garden.

The porch door opened and Mrs P., Benji and Daisy emerged as he got out of the car.

'Before you start shouting it was an accident,' Mrs P. said as they approached.

'I should hope so,' said Palmer. 'I hate to think he did it on purpose.'

'I'm awfully sorry,' came Benji's trembling voice from behind Mrs P., where he had decided it might be safer than within Palmer's reach. 'I really am most terribly sorry, Justin –

I'll have it all repaired, I'll pay for everything. I'm very sorry.'

'What happened?' asked Palmer – although he could see what had happened. But how?

'I lost control.'

Mrs P. thought she could explain it better. 'Benji didn't realise the digger was back wheel drive...'

'So when I turned the steering wheel to the right it went left, through the hedge,' Benji blurted out, wringing his hands in front of him. 'And when I pressed the brake I hit the pedal that lowered the bucket instead and that's what tore up your drive and sent it over on its side. I really am so sorry, Justin.' He was almost in tears.

Mrs P. patted his arm. 'Never mind, Benji – it could have been worse, it could have landed on top of you and killed you!'

'Really?' Palmer nodded. 'Want to have another go?'

****

SATURDAY

'But it's not right guv, we ought to do something about it.' Gheeta was quite adamant.

They were in the Team Room and Gheeta had laid a series of photographs on the table that they had been looking at.

Palmer spread his hands. 'Okay, you're right – there's things that aren't right and should have been questioned at the time. But it's a closed case – it wasn't even classified as a 'crime' case. Those photos don't have Scene of Crime stickers on, do they?'

Claire had walked in and after exchanging 'good mornings' was taking off her coat. She had been to see DS Atkins in Forensic Accounts and collected the report on the turnover increases of the Blooms' business each time a new centre was added.

'What things aren't right?' She peered over Gheeta to the photos. 'Urgh, not nice.'

The photos showed a lady in check shirt and jeans on her back on a concrete floor with a chainsaw resting on her chest. The serious amount of blood around her head and shoulders showed she was very dead.

'Who's that?

'Angela Robinson, Edward Bloom's first wife.'

'Oh right, yes.' Claire remembered the file she had pulled on Edward Bloom's history. 'Chainsaw accident. Is that it?'

'It is,' said Palmer. 'Only the Sergeant doesn't think it was an accident.'

'Look.' Gheeta took a pose as though holding a chainsaw in front of her. 'She's right-handed, so her right hand has the trigger and her left hand would hold the front handle on top of the machine with her fingers on the brake guard in front of it. She's cutting wood and hits a solid metal snag and the chainsaw jumps and severs her jugular artery in the neck. She's dead before she hits the floor. The chain saw falls with her, right?'

Claire nodded. 'Yes.'

'So, it would land on her body and stay there – it wouldn't bounce 'cause it's heavy, one of those industrial ones, not a wood burner owner's type. So explain to me how the chainsaw in the photos has its blade and chain pointing to the right. It would fall pointing to the left, wouldn't it?'

'Yes, not likely to do a complete one hundred and eighty degree turn in the air – no way,' agreed Claire.

'I studied those photos for an hour last night. I knew something was wrong and then it hit me: that chainsaw is definitely pointing the wrong way. It's pointing the correct way if somebody else in front of her had taken it from her and swiped her neck and then thrown or put it down on the body to make it look like an accident. If she dropped it then it's pointing the wrong way'

Claire looked at Palmer. 'Sergeant's right, sir.'

Palmer gave in. 'Okay, write up a cold case review request and I'll pass it on.'

'Let's hope Janet Bloom doesn't decide to cut some wood with a chainsaw, at least not when her husband is around,' said Claire, taking her seat. 'By the way sir, how did Mrs P. get on with Benji yesterday on the rose garden trip?'

'Late cancellation.'

AC Bateman was forty-eight years old, slightly built and the epitome of a social climber in society, but the ladder he was intent on climbing was in the police force; he sucked up to anybody in authority that he thought might assist in his career path towards his ultimate goal of being Commissioner. He was always immaculately turned out in a uniform with ironed creases so sharp they could cut bread.

His nemesis was his head, in that it was bald, totally bald. It didn't worry anybody except AC Bateman, who had tried every remedy advertised to re-thatch his dome: potions, creams, massages and all sorts of oils had failed to deliver on their promised results. It was hereditary; his father had been bald, his brother was bald, and he wasn't sure but he had a suspicion that his elder sister had started to weave false hair pieces into her receding locks at an early age. He had once tried wearing a wig, but the silence from everybody in the Yard on the day he wore it, and the number of staff who kept their hand in front of their faces to cover broad smiles as he walked past put paid to that idea.

There had always been a distrustful undercurrent to Palmer and Bateman's relationship; nothing you could pin down, but Palmer didn't like or agree with fast-tracking of university graduates to management positions in the force. He'd have them do two years on the beat first, see how they handled a seventeen-stone drug dealer waving a ten-inch knife who just did not want to be arrested. Bateman, on the other hand, would like to be surrounded with graduates with '*firsts*' in various '*ologies*', and was very pleased when the government brought in the minimum recruitment requirement of having to have a degree in order to even apply to join the force. He believed the old school coppers like Palmer were outdated dinosaurs, and that crime could be solved by elimination and computer programmes, which is why he had tried unsuccessfully to transfer DS Singh away from Palmer and back into the Cyber Crime Unit from where Palmer had originally poached her. Bateman had no time for an experienced detective's accumulated knowledge being an asset in the war against crime, and the sooner he could shut down the Serial Murder Squad and combine it with the

Organised Crime Unit, CID and Cyber Crime the better. Cutting costs was paramount in Bateman's personal mission statement.

The trouble was that Palmer's team, the Organised Crime Unit, CID and Cyber Crime were producing good case solved figures, which the political masters at the Home Office liked, and they therefore insisted the units carried on working as they were. But what really irked Bateman most of all was that they really liked Palmer too; the press also liked Palmer, and the rank and file loved him. So Bateman managed to keep the false smile on his face as he looked across his plush office on the fifth floor as Palmer took a seat opposite. He put down the daily reports on the case that Gheeta filed religiously, knowing Bateman's obsession with paperwork.

'Are you going to arrest the Blooms, Palmer? Everything seems to be piling up against them – couple of nasty pieces of work by the look of them.'

'I'd like to sir, but it's all circumstantial, nothing that actually pins the murders on them – no fingerprints or DNA in the van, no witnesses, and a story that a good brief would make sound very credible to a jury.'

'The Blooms' car leaving the M25 service area is pretty good circumstantial, Palmer?'

'It is, but the car was reported stolen and that service area is the nearest to where any joy riders who took it from the Blooms might reasonably be expected to head to for a break. No ANPR cameras there.'

'What about the aconite poison? I could issue a search warrant for the Blooms' house?'

'We thought of that sir, but surely they would have more sense than to keep it there. They've got three garden centres where it might justifiably be used and found.'

'Justifiably used?'

'Vermin poison – rats and mice, clears them in no time.'

Bateman pointed to the reports. 'And I see you think all this is tied into a black rose? You'd better enlighten me on that, I'm not a gardener.'

Palmer explained the financial significance of a black rose and the riches to be gained by being the first grower to breed one.

'I don't think it all started out that way,' continued Palmer. 'I think the acquisition of the centres was a way to launder more of the Manchester security van robbery money. As you can see from DS Atkins's remarks on the turnover increases, they are too high to be from organic growth of the business; but when Bloom got wind of Hanley's closeness to breeding a black rose and the money involved in that, he decided he wanted that for himself. The bookkeeper Burnley told Bloom about Hanley's debt and he moved in with an offer to clear it for half the business – the money went through but then something went wrong; maybe Hanley refused to share the rose breeding part of the business. We don't know, but something happened and Bloom killed the Hanleys – of that I'm sure.'

'All right. What I will do is pass the reports over to the CPS and ask them if they think they could prosecute with what we have and let's see what they say.'

Palmer knew the CPS's answer would be 'no way', but Bateman liked to keep his hand on things and make out he was using the right channels and not just pushing paperclips around his desk; even if the channels he used were already fed up with him wasting their time with similar requests in the past.

Palmer nodded and left. He made three cups of espresso coffee at the executive fifth floor Tassimo pod coffee machine before carefully taking the stairs to his second floor and the Team Room, passing the second floor basic 20p-a-time coffee vending machine that had a habit of sending down the cup after the coffee or no cup at all when Palmer used it.

****

'Do you fancy two cold cases, guv?' Gheeta asked him when he returned to the Team Room.

'Two?'

'Charlie Hilton, remember the name?'

'Yes, he was the chap who sold his garden centre in Barnet to the Blooms.'

'Correct.'

'Didn't the chap at the British Association of Rose Breeders think it was all legal?'

'He didn't know what we know about the Blooms, guv.'

Palmer sat down and paid full attention. 'Go on.'

'Well, whilst you were upstairs with Mr Bateman I thought I'd have a word with Mr Hilton's solicitor, so I checked with Companies House and he was listed on the change of owner documentation and luckily he's still in practice. Guess what?'

'Oh, come on – don't get all theatrical or I'll transfer you to Latin at the morgue and you can form a double act.'

Gheeta and Claire laughed.

'The short version of it is that the Blooms were going into a fifty-fifty partnership with Charlie Hilton. Sound familiar?

'Very familiar. Go on.'

'And then he died – heart attack. He had a history of heart problems and had two attacks in the previous year, which was the main reason why he wanted to retire. Anyway, straight away after his death the Blooms offered to buy the centre outright; the deal for the partnership had gone through, just as the chap from the BARB said, all thoroughly legal, and the Blooms were fifty percent owners, so when they offered to buy the lot it made sense for the Hilton family to accept as neither the wife nor Charlie's two grown-up children were interested in it and the deal went through without a hitch. Funny how he had a heart attack at that particular time; even his solicitor said it happened at the right time and the family were very grateful to the Blooms.'

'If I recall what Latin told us, aconite overpowers the heart and stops it.'

'Correct, guv.'

'Give him a call and see if the poison remains in the body and would show up on an exhumation.'

'On Charlie Hilton?'

'Yes.'

'Cremated – I checked.'

'Damn.'

'The other thing I checked was DS Atkins's report on the Blooms' accounts before and after their acquisitions of other centres. Charlie Hilton's garden centre's last accounts before his death showed a turnover of four hundred and seventy thousand that year; first year in the Blooms' hands their accounts showed an increase in turnover of just under two million, and the only addition to their business was Hilton's centre. Hardly likely for them to increase its turnover by nearly one and a half million in a year.'

'More of the Manchester security van proceeds being washed.'

'Seems likely, guv – and there is another interesting side to Hilton's business.'

'Oh, what's that?'

'Guess who his bookkeeper was?'

Palmer didn't need a second guess. 'She wasn't, was she?'

'According to the Hiltons' solicitor she was – and she was very, very helpful, his words, on getting the deal with the Blooms done and dusted.'

Palmer rubbed his chin in thought. 'Alison Burnley seems to be manoeuvring herself into a position of *accomplice to murder*.'

'Well, she's either part of the team or she's incredibly stupid. She's seen four people who got involved with Bloom in a business deal die, either during or a short time after the deal is done. It must have raised questions in her mind surely?'

'As bookkeeper to the Blooms she would have seen the increase in turnover each time – a big increase after Angela Robinson died and an increase far in excess of what the added Hilton garden centre would bring in organic growth. No, she's got to be part of it.'

'Or maybe Bloom has some sort of hold over her?'

Palmer looked at Claire. 'Burnley hasn't got a criminal record, has she?' He knew Claire would have checked.

'Clean as a new whistle, sir.'

****

Jim Riley sat in his bedsit pondering his position; still nothing in the local paper about the Hanleys' deaths. He really didn't know what to do, his mind was all over the place.

A knock at his door interrupted his thoughts.

'Who is it?

'Me, Alison.'

'You alone?'

'Yes.'

He slipped the chain and let Alison Burnley in. She took the nearest armchair and sat regaining her breath. 'Jesus, Jim... Your stairs are worse than the ones to my office...'

'What do you want?'

She waved away his request as she lit a cigarette and slouched back in the chair. 'Give me a minute to get my breath back,' she wheezed, taking a long drag.

'If Bloom sent you, you're wasting your time. Murderers, the pair of them.'

'You can't prove that Jim, nobody can – not even the police.'

'They told me. They poisoned the Hanleys.'

That had an effect on Burnley who sat bolt upright. 'Poisoned?'

'Aconite, fed it to them in a drink.'

'Christ, not another one.' She slumped back.

It was Jim's turn to sit bolt upright. 'Another one? What do you mean another one?'

'They killed Charlie Hilton that way.'

'What?!'

'He was quite happy doing a partnership with them, and then when it was done they poisoned him with aconite; nobody questioned it, he'd a history of heart attacks and the doc said that's what it was. Soon as the funeral was over the Blooms stepped in with an offer for the rest of the business which Charlie's family accepted.'

'If you knew this why didn't you tell the police?'

'I couldn't, I'd go to prison. Look at me Jim, do you think I'd last ten minutes inside?'

'Why would you go to prison? Are you working with Bloom? Are you part of it?'

'God no, no! I didn't know Edward Bloom until he came to work for Angela Robinson. I had a feeling he was no good and I was right – they said her death was accidental, but it bloody well wasn't. I can't prove anything, but no way would Angela have an accident with a chainsaw – for Christ's sake, the thing had an emergency stop on it! Police weren't interested and coroner gave an accidental death verdict.' She took a long drag. 'I couldn't say anything Jim, because I'd been milking Angela's bank account for years – not a big amount but a couple of thousand a month, putting through fake invoices and making cheques out to myself instead of the names on the invoices. She trusted me and I betrayed that trust. Bloom cottoned onto what

I was doing and has held it over me ever since – I daren't go to the police.'

'Were you stealing from the Hanleys too?'

Burnley took a deep breath. 'Yes, and of course Bloom guessed that. If I was doing it to one, I would be doing it to all: Angela, Charlie Hilton and the Hanleys. I'd go down for a long time, Jim.'

'You deserve to, you thief.'

'Yes, I can imagine how you feel Jim – I really am very sorry, I wish to God I'd never started. But it was so easy and I could go abroad instead of Bournemouth, buy nice things – it just took hold of me. I knew it was wrong but I couldn't stop, and when Bloom told me he knew, I was scared; one word from him and I was sunk. So you can see that in my position I have to back the Blooms, otherwise my life's basically going to end in a prison. If you go to the police about the poison and the black rose and the Blooms get arrested, it will all come out – Edward said he'd see me inside with him. You can't do that to me Jim, you can't.'

Riley stood up. 'Get out.'

'What?'

'Get out – go on, get out! You deserve to go down, same as Bloom. I'll see the pair of you behind bars, and good riddance if you die inside.'

Burnley's mood changed to offensive. 'You'll go down too Jim, you're as much a thief as me – you're the one giving Bloom the black rose plants and cuttings you stole from Hanley. It's Chelsea Flower Show this coming Monday as you know, and they're unveiling the black rose on the Bloom stand during the royal visit – the mother plant is in bloom and it will be the sensation of the show. Bloom won't let you ruin that, no way.'

'Thieving a rose from Hanley is hardly the same as stealing thousands from his bank account, is it? I don't care anyway, I'll admit it and get a short sentence. It's not murder is it, and it's not knowing about a murder and keeping quiet either, is it? Get out.'

'Bloom will say you are part of the plan – he'll say you are in it up to your eyes. He'll take you down with him. Think about it, Jim.'

'Get out.'

He went to the door and held it open for Burnley to leave.

'And don't come back. I don't want to see you again, except in court.'

Burnley stubbed out her cigarette on a saucer and heaved herself out of the chair. 'You might regret it if you go to the police,

Jim. Bloom's not the sort of man to cross; he's got a criminal record you know, so you may want to think carefully about what you do. Don't be rash, it's your future as well as mine.' She walked out onto the landing and the door slammed behind her without any further words between them.

Burnley made her way carefully down the stairs, out onto the street and across the road to where Edward Bloom was sat waiting for her in his car. She slumped into the passenger seat took her cigarette packet from her shoulder bag and pulled one out.

Bloom snatched it from her hand and threw it out of the window. 'No smoking in the car. What did he say?'

'He's going to the police in the morning.'

'Did you tell him what I said to tell him?'

'Yes, I told him he'd be in the frame as well, that you'd implicate him and you're not the sort of person to cross.'

'And?'

'Didn't make any difference. He's going to blow the whole thing apart in the morning.'

'Oh no he's not, he's not going to ruin our unveiling of the black rose at Chelsea – no way is he going to stop that. Get out.'

'What?'

'Get out – I said out! Get the bus home or grab a taxi. I'm going to sort out Jim Riley. Go on, out.'

'What do you mean *you're going to sort him out*?' asked Burnley as she struggled her large body back out of the car.

'Just that – I'm going to sort him out once and for all. Now go'

****

From his front window in the bedsit Jim watched as Burnley crossed the road and got into Bloom's car. A short time later she got out again and walked off. He was getting angry but his anger was tempered with guilt. His mobile rang.

'Hello.'

'It's Alison.' Her voice was shaking. 'Watch your back, Jim – Bloom's coming up and he said he was *going to sort you out once and for all*. I told you he's got previous – I'd get out the back way if there is one. What have we got ourselves into, Jim?'

He didn't answer. He finished the call and stood looking down at the Bloom car. The Hanleys had been good to him; he had a good job which he liked, they'd stood as security for him for the bedsit rent, and if he ever wanted time off he got it. He watched as Edward Bloom got out of the car. So he was going to *sort him out*, was he? He'd guessed Burnley had just been a messenger and he'd guessed right; she was backed into a corner by Bloom and his knowledge of her financial embezzlements and couldn't move. He watched as Bloom went to the car boot and took something out and slid it up his right jacket sleeve before crossing the road towards the bedsit entrance stairs – a knife? Riley's heart upped a pace; he was getting more and more angry. What had Bloom in mind? Stab him to death and hope the police thought it was a burglar he'd disturbed? Okay Edward Bloom, if that's the way you want to play it then that's the way I'll play it too.

He had to think fast. There was an old fire escape at the end of the short landing outside the bedsit but God only knows when that was last opened, or even if it did open – Jim's landlord wasn't exactly on top of the Health and Safety regulation demands. No, he had to take on Bloom, but he had an advantage knowing Bloom was on his way up; he needed to use that advantage, especially if Bloom had a weapon of some sort.

Jim thought quickly and opened the door a couple of inches and stood pressed against the wall behind it so that he wouldn't be seen by anybody opening it. He waited.

'Jim, are you there?' Bloom called his name from outside the door.

'Yes, who is it?' replied Jim.

The door opened slowly and when Bloom stepped alongside it Jim struck. He barged his shoulder against the door as hard as he could; it sideswiped Bloom and knocked him off balance sideways so he stumbled and fell against the armchair, a short steel rod falling out of his jacket sleeve. Jim was out and down the stairs like greased lightning; he ran up the street, dodging between the shoppers until he was a good hundred metres away from the bedsit entrance and only then turning to look back. Bloom wasn't in sight.

Jim slipped into a shop doorway and watched. It was a couple of minutes before he saw Bloom come out of the bedsit entrance and cross to his car. He was limping; good, that will slow him down a bit. To Jim's consternation Bloom didn't get in the car and drive off; he was just composing himself, rubbing his right knee and looking up and down the busy street. What would he do now?

Jim waited. Shit! Bloom crossed back onto Jim's side of the street and started coming his way, looking into the shops as he came. Jim tried to blend with the shoppers and continued walking up the road. After another fifty metres he took a glance round; Bloom was still coming, and at that moment, a hundred metres apart, their eyes met. Bloom started to move faster, as fast as his limp would allow.

Jim ran; his car was parked in a side road the other way from the bedsit. He took the next left off the main street and then the next left again, and then again which brought him into the road where his car was. Panting like a dog in the hot sun he slumped into the driver's seat and took stock of things. He couldn't go back to the bedsit and the garden centre was out of the question; he needed time, time to calm down and gather his thoughts. He turned the ignition key and the engine started. He took a look in the rear view mirror – all clear, no Edward Bloom in sight.

Then the passenger window splintered into a million pieces of glass, showering him and the front seats; through the empty space where it had been he saw Bloom raising the steel rod ready to smash it through the windscreen. Jim grated into gear – any gear would do – and floored the accelerator. The car responded by leaping forward, its tyres screaming their protest and the gears shouting to be shifted up. In the mirror he could see Bloom stumbling after him, hampered by his limp; he threw the steel bar after the car in anger but it fell short as Jim's foot was still pressing the accelerator to the floor and had put some distance between them.

Jim prayed that the traffic in the main street would be moving and not at a halt. He was in luck, it was moving and he pulled out of the side street into it and away. Bloom would soon be back to his car and after him, so he took the next right and then zigzagged down roads he had never been to before; turn right, next left, next right, next left, straight on – he didn't know where he was and didn't care, as long as Bloom's car didn't show in his rear view mirror. After a while he hit the Edgware Road and knew where he was. He needed a place to stay that night, so he turned into Praed Street – plenty of B&Bs here. He turned into the side streets and soon found one with a small car park; he managed to park close against a wall so his missing window wouldn't draw attention. He tidied up the front seats and pushed the broken glass under them out of sight and then booked into a single room.

Flopping onto the bed his mind was whirring with a mixture of remorse and anger; a plan of revenge was already forming – a bloody good plan too. He laughed as he thought about how the plan would work. Burnley telling him that the Blooms were unveiling the black rose at Chelsea on Monday had stopped any thoughts of going to the police. If he had gone to the police it would take a few days for them to check his story and arrest Bloom. No, he had to act alone. The black rose was Geoff Hanley's and Bloom was not going to get it – Jim had worked out the ultimate twist. He laughed again as he thought about it – brilliant, bloody brilliant!

****

Palmer couldn't park on his drive as the workmen that Benji had hired to do the repairs had their tools and cement mixers on it. The deep gash had been filled and half the herringbone pattern bricks replaced; he was impressed with how much they'd managed in one day. The hole in the hedge through to Benji's garden had been tidied, but the jagged path the digger's wide tyres had made as it slewed through Mrs P.'s rose bed was still there.

He parked on the road at the end of his drive and walked up it as Mrs P. came out.

'Don't hang about, do they?' he said as she joined him.

'They haven't stopped all day, no lunch break. I think Benji must have put them on a time bonus.'

They both laughed.

Palmer pointed to the gap in the hedge. 'What about the hole in the hedge? You going to get something strong and sturdy to plant there?'

'Well, I was thinking about that. How about a gate?'

'A gate?'

'Yes, I mean Benji's always popping in with some problem or other – you know what he's like – and it would make it easier for me when I go round to help in his garden. I thought a nice steel gate, nothing elaborate. What do you think would go nicely there?'

'Razor wire.'

'That's not very neighbourly, Justin.'

'He's a walking disaster! So far this year he's burnt down part of the garden fence with his barbeque, flooded the front garden when his hot tub collapsed, and now this. I hate to think what's next.'

A sharp bang from the road caught their attention. Benji's brand new Kia Sorento was slewed across the front of Palmer's CRV where he had turned in towards his drive; Palmer's offside wing mirror and Benji's nearside wing mirror both hung limply from their fastenings. A somewhat distraught Benji was hurrying towards them.

'I'm sorry, I'm really sorry – I'm not used to having you parked there and I didn't leave enough room when I turned into my drive. It's only the wing mirror Justin, no damage to the car, I'll get it replaced. I'm so very sorry!'

****

Gheeta's current boy friend Jaz was waiting at foot of her Barbican apartment block waving a takeaway as she parked up.

'What have we got?'

'Thai.'

'Sounds good to me.'

In the apartment Gheeta took a quick shower and put on a bathrobe as Jaz set the table and put the food in the oven on a low gas to keep hot.

'Oh no,' Gheeta pointed to the computer, the Zoom indicator was flashing. 'I forgot it's Saturday, family chat day.'

'It's okay, the food's in the oven it can wait.' He moved out of camera shot and sat down watching the activity on the Thames below as the tourist boats took their last trips of the day and the freight barges moved slowly down towards the docks.

Family chat day was the weekly evening internet get together of Gheeta, her mum from home in South London and her aunt Raani and cousin Bervinder in New York.

Gheeta clicked in. 'Hello mum, Aunty Raani, Bervinder, you all okay?'

They all were. 'Are you busy dear?' mum asked. 'We missed you last week?'

'Yes, always busy mum, crime never stops.'

'This is not a career for a young lady, no,' Aunt Raani was shaking her head. 'You should go and work with your family that is far better.'

Gheeta's family had a large computer parts supply company built by her father and both her elder brothers were in the business as well. Her father had made it clear that at any time she could join the firm in an executive position and quite often her IT expertise had been called on to test their products.

'I'm very happy doing what I am doing Aunt Raani, I love my job you know that.' She'd been down this path with Aunt Raani many times.

'You should be loving a husband and children at your age Gheeta, not loving a job your mother could find a suitable man.'

Gheeta's mum laughed, 'I could, I could probably find quite a few *suitable men,* but I won't.'

'What case are you working on Gheeta?' Bavinder asked changing the subject. She held her elder cousin in awe and had already at age 16 made up her mind she was joining the NYPD and from there moving into the

FBI. But that couldn't happen until she reached the minimum seventeen and half year age requirement and if Aunt Raani had her way it would never happen, an arranged marriage would happen, both Gheeta and Bavinder knew that wasn't ever going to happen.

'Murder in the greenhouse,' laughed Gheeta answering Bavinder's question.

'What!

'Well, it would take too long to explain but basically a Garden Center owner has bred a rare plant and others are prepared to kill to get it.'

'Kill for a plant?' Bavinder didn't understand.

'A plant worth a million pounds and maybe more.'

'Oh wow!!' Bavinder understood now. 'How many dead so far?'

Aunt Raani interrupted waving her hand, 'This is not a suitable conversation for a young lady, tell me Gheeta are you still going out with that nice young man Jaz?'

Jaz looked up and met Gheeta's eye with a surprised look.

'Yes, he's still around,' Gheeta said nonchalantly and smiled as Jaz's surprised expression faded.

'Has your mother and father met him?' Aunt Raani was on her favourite subject.

'Several times,' said Gheeta's mum. 'And we like him.'

Jaz wet his finger drew an invisible 1 in the air and gave Gheeta a large 'so there' smile.

Aunt Raani wasn't impressed, 'But he is only a car salesman you can do better than that Gheeta, much better.'

Gheeta got her own back on Jaz, 'Yes, yes I suppose I could, I'll keep looking Aunt Raani.'

Gheeta's mum came to Jaz's rescue. 'He is not a car salesman Raani, his family own three Mercedes and two BMW dealerships, he's not standing on a second hand car lot in the Old Kent Road looking like Arthur Daly!'

'Who is Arthur Daly, do we know his family?' asked Raani.

'Never mind,' Gheeta's mum said through her laughter, she was fed up with her sister's old fashioned and outdated ideas about arranged marriages and family liaisons. 'Are you going to tell Bavinder who she should marry when the time comes?'

Aunt Raani nodded, 'I will make suggestions yes.'

'You can make as many suggestions as you like mum,' Bavinder said, 'But I won't be listening. When mister right comes along, *if* mister right comes along I'm grabbing him with or without your stamp of approval.'

'And when the one you grab isn't mister right and it all breaks down then you will wish you had asked your mother's opinion.' Aunt Raani sat back with a shake of her head.

'No I won't, I'll divorce him and grab another mister right!' Bavinder laughed. 'Anyway I'm not going to get married, I've told you a thousand times mum, I'm joining the NYPD in a year's time when I'm seventeen and a half and then I'll be working my way up and into the FBI.'

Aunt Raani shook her head, this was a battle she wouldn't win and she knew it. 'You'll both end up as spinsters you and Gheeta, sad and lonely in your old age.'

'No mum, I'll end up as boss of the FBI and Gheeta will end up as Commissioner of the Met.'

Gheeta laughed, 'I don't think that's very likely for me but I wouldn't be at all surprised if you got there Bavinder.'

Aunt Raani waved her hands negatively, 'No, no, no don't encourage her Gheeta, where am I going to get my grandchildren from?'

Gheeta's mum smiled, 'You should have had more children yourself if that's what you want.'

Aunt Raani looked to the Heavens in despair, 'You think the one child I have isn't enough trouble, you think I want more? You are very lucky sister, Gheeta has two brothers who have given you grandchildren all I have is Bavinder who gives me heart ache and worry.'

Gheeta was feeling hungry, 'I have to go I've got a meal in the oven and a load of reports to write.' A little white lie never hurt anybody.

They said their goodbyes and Gheeta switched off.

Jaz stood up and smiled, 'Your mum likes me.'

Gheeta smiled back, 'Don't get ahead of yourself Arthur.'

'Arthur?'

'Arthur Daly, I'm going to call you *Arfur* from now on.'

'Oh, so there is a *from now on then*?'

'Gheeta waved an admonishing finger, 'Don't get ahead of yourself *Arfur*, you know the rules, come when you're called and go when you're told to.'

'Yes ma'am.'

****

SUNDAY

Jim Riley watched the local early morning news on the TV in his room at the B&B; nothing about the Hanleys but lots about tomorrow's Chelsea Flower Show and the royal opening, with Monty Don talking to excited exhibitors as they put the final touches to their displays and show gardens. The Blooms weren't included.

After a good full English breakfast Jim paid his bill and drove to the Hanley Garden Centre. The staff were waiting outside as he pulled into the car park; Edward Bloom was nowhere to be seen. Jim let them in and shut the main door; there was half an hour until opening time so he called the staff together and explained that Mr Hanley was ill and staying at home, and that he, Jim, had a family problem he had to take care of and wouldn't be in for the weekend. He gave the cashier the keys and left the centre in her capable hands. He had one thing to do today ready for his plan to work tomorrow.

He left his car at the centre; if Bloom came there looking for him and the car was there, Bloom might think he'd be coming back for it. He wouldn't be.

He walked a fair distance away from the centre, keeping a wary eye out for Bloom, and then made his way to an internet cafe where he booked the minimum fifteen minutes with use of a printer and completed the final part of his plan. He checked the page he had typed as it came out of the printer; it looked good, very good. He smiled to himself, thinking of Janet

Bloom's face when she saw it; the smile broke into a laugh.

He bought a strong card folder and Sellotape from the local WHSmiths and sat in a cafe with a coffee and carefully stuck the paper to the card. Now he had the rest of the day to himself; he couldn't go back to the bedsit – too dangerous and an obvious place that Bloom would check – so he jumped on a bus to the West End and spent the afternoon wandering around the shops, until he took a black cab across the river to Waterloo and booked into another bedsit. He thought that was far enough away from the centres and Bloom wouldn't find him if he was looking. He was happy that he'd covered his tracks.

****

Earlier that day Gheeta came into the Team Room where Palmer was going through the reports and Claire was digging away at the Blooms' pasts.

Palmer looked up and put the papers down. 'Well, what has he found out then?'

Gheeta had been over to Reg Frome's forensics unit where Peter Akins had brought her up-to-date on some new abnormalities that he had found as he dug deeper into the Hanley accounts.

'Well, it appears Miss Burnley has had her fingers in the till for a long time – in fact right from the start of her involvement with the Hanleys. And it wasn't just her fingers in the till, she had both hands in there. Atkins estimates she embezzled about twelve thousand a year.'

'Without Hanley realising?' Palmer was amazed.

'Oh she's a crafty one, guv. Geoff Hanley wasn't a money man at all – left it all to her. He used to sign all the cheques in a book and left her to get on with it, and that seems to have been the extent of his interest in the finances of the garden centre.'

'Preoccupied with his roses, I suppose.'

'Probably. What do you want me to do, get a warrant and bring her in?'

'Not yet – seems she isn't *clean as a whistle* after all. I get the feeling Miss Burnley might hold the key to open up this case and what the Bloom's have been up to. Let her run for a while longer.'

'Jim Riley might hold that key too, sir,' said Claire as she sat back in her chair and turned towards them. 'Guess who was on the same horticultural course and in the same year as him at Pershore College?'

'Alan Titchmarsh?' joked Palmer.

'Quite possibly sir, but of more interest to us, Janet Bloom was – or as she was then, Janet Jones.'

'Really? So they go back a few years then.'

'She passed out with Distinction and double A, and Jim with a B plus.'

'This is becoming a real can of worms, isn't it? Burnley wasn't the college bookkeeper, was she?'

'Not as far as I can see by the records, sir,' laughed Claire.

'Shame, that really would be a turn up for the books wouldn't it?'

'Hang on a minute guv, bells are ringing.' Gheeta sat at her keyboard and typed away for a couple of minutes and then scrolled down looking for something. 'Got it. I thought the name rang a bell.'

'Got what?'

'Well, according to the HMRC records for Angela Robinson's garden centre, a *Janet Jones* was on the payroll there for two years before Edward Bloom inherited it.'

Claire stood and looked over Gheeta's shoulder at the screen. 'That's the same year as she left college. So she went straight to work for Angela Robinson.'

'And there she met Mr Edward Bloom,' added Palmer. 'The final bits of the jigsaw are falling into place.'

Gheeta rose and went to the progress board at the end of the room and taking a felt tip drew arrowed lines from Angela Robinson's photo to Edward Bloom and to Janet Bloom writing *'née Jones'* below her, and then drawing a line between Janet and Edward Bloom and another from Janet Bloom to Jim Riley.

'Looking more like a proper crime road map now, guv.' She finished off by putting lines from Alison Burnley to Hanley, Robinson and Bloom.

****

MONDAY

Jim Riley was up bright and early; in fact he hadn't slept much that night. The plan was going round and round in his mind. He was first down to the breakfast room and scoured the national papers. No, still nothing about the Hanleys, and the news on the TV in the breakfast room didn't mention them either. So the police *must* think it was just suicide. Well, they wouldn't after today, oh no...

He collected the folder from his room, paid his bill and left. He hailed a black cab to take him to Watford and got out a few hundred yards up the road from Bloom's Garden Centre; being a Sunday the area wasn't that busy. He checked his mobile for the time: eight thirty. Good, no staff would be in the centre for at least half an hour, and that was all the time he needed. He let himself in through the staff door and made his way to the rose house, checking all the time to make sure he was alone. Mind you, when staff arrived they wouldn't be bothered about him; they all knew who he was and had seen him at the centre many times with Edward Bloom.

In the rose house he made his way to the far end corner benches where the black rose plants and cuttings were still in their neat lines where he had put them after bringing them from Hanley's after Bloom's threats in the bedsit. As he walked towards them he put down his folder and took a pair of shears from a bench. Standing still for a moment, he took a deep breath. 'This is for you Geoff,' he said softly, and worked his way along the bench cutting through the plants' stems and sweeping them and their pots off the bench clattering down onto the concrete floor. The pots of cuttings and bud wood followed. He was feeling good, almost elated by the act of destroying the plants. It felt right; the guilt about the Hanleys was evaporating.

The feeling was brought to a shuddering halt as a shout came from the door.

'Hey! What do you think you're doing?!'

Jim looked over his shoulder and saw the figure of Edward Bloom running between the benches towards him as fast as his limp would allow. Jim carried on cutting and slicing the stems as fast as he could.

'You little bastard, I'll kill you! Stop it!' Bloom shouted getting nearer. Jim could hear the uneven steps of Bloom's limp were nearly on him. He turned to face him with the closed shears as protection.

Bloom was too near; the limping leg hadn't the strength to stop him. His eyes widened with horror as he realised that and impaled himself on the shears, his face jerking forwards to within an inch of Jim's, and then he sank to the floor where he lay on his back with the shears embedded deep into his chest and heart, the handles sticking up like masts on a ship. Jim stood speechless, watching the bubbling froth coming from Bloom's mouth turn red and the body settle limply onto the concrete as more red spread across it.

It was an accident, Jim told himself again and again; it was an accident, he didn't mean to kill him, it happened so quickly, an accident. The police wouldn't believe that – they'd think it was murder, of course they would. He had to go – he could run; he wouldn't get far, he knew that, but he had to get out of there. He had the plan – yes, the plan. He picked up the folder; he had to complete his plan then hand himself in – but the plan had to go ahead, had to. He left by the staff door, nodding to several staff members who were arriving. It wouldn't be long before Bloom's body was found, and they'd seen him there so the police would be after him. He checked his clothes – they were clean, no blood. That's good. He walked quickly away from the centre and called for an Uber on his mobile.

****

Palmer checked his watch: ten o'clock. The call from the Control Room had come through to him at home at nine; he had just returned with Daisy from a walk to the newsagent to pick up the paper. Benji's workmen were already on the drive setting the bricks in place with Benji fussing round like a mother hen, worried that a brick might be half a bubble out. In the end Mrs P., who could see the workmen were getting rather cheesed off with him, had called him in for a coffee and advised him to let them get on with it.

She was rather glad when the Control Room phoned and Palmer was soon whisked away by a patrol car. Bad enough with Benji in a state of permanent panic without Palmer putting his oar in with non-helpful remarks.

'Toad in the hole tonight,' she shouted after him as he ran down the drive – well, half a drive anyway.

'Beef sausages, not veggie,' he shouted back.

Now he stood in the Bloom's Watford Centre rose house watching as the OIC had the area taped off and forensics moved in with cameras and tape measures.

Reg Frome stood beside him. 'You realise we are going to have to fingerprint all those broken pots – every damn bit of them.'

Palmer shook his head. 'No, no don't bother Reg – just the shears. Riley was seen by witnesses leaving the place, I think you'll find they're his prints on it. Sergeant Singh's taking their initial statements now. I've put out a call to pick him up if we can find him. There's a TSG Unit checking his bedsit but I don't think he'll go there, bit too obvious.'

Sergeant Singh joined them. 'Right, that's four witnesses who saw Riley leaving – none saw him arrive so I would guess he came in early, he must have a key to the staff door.

What do you want to do about telling Janet Bloom what's happened? Apparently she's at the Chelsea Flower Show today as it's the royal visit and press preview day. I've told the staff not to contact her or talk about what happened to anybody as it's best left to a FLO to break the news gently, and I've sent them all home until they get a call from us. I've got the local uniforms putting up crime scene tape sealing off the centre.'

'Good, well done. The Path boys will be here soon to take the body to the morgue; it's obviously not an accidental death so Professor Latin will have to do a PM. Nothing else we can do here so we had better get over to Chelsea in case Riley goes for Janet Bloom, although he didn't strike me as the type to deliberately kill somebody.'

'Nor me guv, but…' She pointed at Bloom's body. 'Maybe we are both wrong?'

****

The Royal Hospital Road was busy with tourists and people who had made the journey to try and catch a glimpse of the Queen as she arrived at the show for the royal preview.

Riley blended in and left the crowd at the main gate, walking on and around the block to the back entrance where the garden builders, staff and the plants and trees went in. He had timed it right; many workers were strolling out for lunch and others hurrying back to complete the last minute tasks, hoping to impress the judges and the royal party. Security at the wide gates was lax, too many ins and outs to check tags and passes. Jim held his folder like a management trainee trying to impress and slipped in amongst a returning group of builders as they walked through the gates exchanging banter with the two guards. Once in the complex and a good distance from the gates, Jim left the group and made his way along the main concourse. He blended well with the folder held purposefully in his hand as he passed the gardeners and their sponsors, all exhibiting the last-minute irrational behaviour of people sure that they have forgotten something but can't think what.

At the top of the main concourse was the huge main marquee housing the trade stands, and somewhere inside was the Bloom stand. Jim walked in; it was busy inside, the same underlying atmosphere of mild panic as apparent as it was outside. The royal party had arrived, the deferential meet and greets, curtseys and bows had been made, and now HRH was on her way slowly up the concourse. The news of her arrival had spread and most of the people in the marquee crowded in the doorway hoping for a glimpse.

Jim walked along the outside row of display stands. He took a discarded cap off a wheelbarrow parked between two stands and put it on, pulling it down at the front in case CCTV was operational. A narrow access walkway ran between the back of the stands and the side of the marquee; Jim turned quickly between two unattended stands and entered the walkway. Avoiding the discarded plant pots, pallets and half empty bags of display grit and composts he moved along it, checking through the stands' back sheets looking for Bloom's stand. His heart nearly stopped a couple of times as he passed employees coming the other way or still arranging displays for their companies, but the firmly held folder in his hand worked a treat and gave him a degree of 'management status' as he passed them with a curt nod of the head.

And then he was there: the back of the Bloom's stand. He knew it was theirs by the rubbish and empty pots in the walkway behind it, pots with Hanley's stickers still in place. Jim felt a twist of anger in his body at seeing them.

'Her Majesty's halfway along now.'

He heard a female voice and very slightly moving the side of the black back drape to the stand he peeped through. Janet Bloom and two of her staff were giving the front shelves of the stand a last-minute soft brush.

Janet Bloom put her brush down. 'Okay, nothing else we can do now ladies. Let's go and have a quick look at the royal party and then get changed – I need to freshen up a bit anyway, come on. Give me your brushes, I'll get rid of them round the back.'

He'd had it! She'd find him there. Jim frantically looked around, but there was nothing big enough to hide behind. If she saw him, he would just have to run. He watched the end of the stand, waiting for Janet Bloom to come round the corner. She didn't; her hand did and threw the brushes towards the rest of the rubbish. Jim sat down and breathed deeply as he regained his composure. He gave Janet and her helpers a minute to get far enough away from the stand and then stood up again, peeping through the back sheet. He saw what he was looking for: slap bang in the middle of the stand, on top of a jet black plinth, stood a large plant in its pot covered by a light jet black fleece. Jim didn't need to look to know what plant was under that fleece waiting for the big royal reveal! He couldn't go to the front of the stand for fear of being seen; he had to put the final part of his plan into operation from the back.

He bent and slipped under the back sheet and slowly stood up and reached forward to the black fleece, and raising it a little way he pulled the Bloom's sign away from the front of it. He read it: *'**The Queen**, the first black rose, bred by Edward and Janet Bloom and dedicated to Her Majesty Queen Elizabeth II.'*

Jim put the sign in his folder and pulled out the one he had made at the internet cafe and replaced the Blooms' sign with it. Quickly he put the fleece back in position and then slipped back under the back sheet to the walkway. He ought to get out of the place now, get away as far as he could; the body of Edward must have been found and police would be looking for him after the staff at the Watford centre told them he had been there. He had one last part to the plan, but he couldn't resist seeing this part play out, he just couldn't.

He kept to the walkway and followed it round to the opposite end of the marquee. The noise was growing; he peeked into the main part and saw the royal party were walking slowly in. They moved along the row of stands, the stand owners hoping for a few words, but only one or two got a brief acknowledgement or nod of the head and a smile as she went by. Behind the royal party a row of security officers, plainclothes and uniformed police kept the following press horde at a respectable twenty metres distance. Jim tagged on behind them with the public. He spied Janet Bloom coming out of the staff only rest room into the main hall and hurrying to her stand. She had changed into a jet-black trouser suit with patent black high heels, and a wide black hair band tied back her blonde hair. Her two assistants had also changed into black skirts and jackets with the Bloom logo embroidered on them. The black wasn't in mourning for Edward that was for sure, so Janet couldn't know of his death? The body must have been found by now surely? Jim was confused.

He kept the cap pulled down and his heart lost a beat again as Janet Bloom gave her stand a last good look as Her Majesty moved to the adjacent one, and then at last to the

Blooms' stand. She must have been primed that something was going to happen at this stand as the whole royal party stopped and the Queen said a few words to Janet after the perfunctory curtseys from her and her assistants. Then they all turned towards the display and an assistant went to the side and slowly pulled the nylon line that raised the fleece.

And there it was, the first mature black rose ever bred. A ripple of applause went through the crowd and very quickly died; but not as quick as Janet Bloom's wide smile died on her lips. Everybody could see the rose, and everybody could see Jim's sign in broad black font:

*'**Midnight Glory**' bred by Geoff Hanley and stolen by Edward and Janet Bloom who then murdered the Hanleys.*

Chaos, disorder and confusion hit the royal party, the press and the public as they read it. The press were the first to react, pushing through the royal security ring to get close-up pictures of the rose and the sign before battering a stunned Janet Bloom with pertinent questions.

'Did you steal it, Mrs Bloom?'

'Who's Geoff Hanley?'

'What's all that about a murder?'

'Have you murdered somebody for the rose?'

'Is it your rose, Mrs Bloom?'

The countless flashlights from the cameras trained on the rose and on Janet Bloom merged into one continual white glow lighting up the marquee. The Royal Protection Unit had the Queen away and into the staff area immediately and the show security staff helped Janet Bloom and her assistants fight through the throng to the same exit.

Jim Riley worked his way to the back of the crowd, out of the Marquee and along the concourse to the entrance and exit. He needed to get away, well away. There was a final part to his plan, and he needed to just book in somewhere for the night and compose himself. So far so good, but the final part was the part where it could all backfire.

****

'We are going to have to give them something, Justin. The phones are going mad.'

Lucy Price, the head of Media and Press at the Yard, was standing in the Team Room with Palmer and Gheeta. They had just got back from the Watford garden centre and the Chelsea Flower Show debacle had hit the news.

'I can't keep this under wraps for long, the journos know there's something big going on; they've checked the Blooms' Watford centre and the Hanley one and they're both closed with a uniform presence. This won't go away Justin, not with HRH being there at the time – tonight's new will have pictures and tomorrow's papers will probably all lead on it, it's a big story. I need a holding statement to see us through until tomorrow, and then I'll need a press briefing.'

Palmer knew they had to give out something. 'Okay, I understand. DS Singh will bring you up to speed and you can work out a statement to release. I have to get over to the morgue, Professor Latin wants to see me about Edward Bloom's body. He seems to have got to work on it pretty quickly, something's excited him. Keep the statement brief Lucy, no names – I don't want Riley doing a runner. Just something along the lines that after the Chelsea fiasco we have started an investigation into the Hanleys, who we understand are on holiday.'

'We can't lie, Justin. If that came back and bit us both you and I would be down the Job Centre.'

'Okay, then how about we are already looking into the mysterious deaths of the Hanleys and will hold a press conference tomorrow once we have more information? That should do it.'

'All right, we'll go with that one. Come on Gheeta, I'll get that out and then you can fill me in on what's really happening.'

Price and Singh left the room with Palmer; he had a car waiting to take him to the morgue and they went off to the Media Centre.

****

'It wasn't murder.' Professor Latin was adamant shaking his head. 'It wasn't murder, Justin.'

'Okay, explain.' Palmer prepared himself for another theatrical experience. He stood beside Latin in the morgue, wearing the required green plastic oversuit, overshoes, hat and mask. Edward Bloom's body lay stretched out on a steel bench in front of them; the shears were in an evidence bag beside it, Frome having taken the prints off them and sent them by police motorcyclist for running through the National Data programme for a match. Palmer had no doubt whose they would match.

'The shears were plunged into the body with both the person holding them and the victim standing in an upright position. In that scenario two things are apparent: one, they would have penetrated only a short way because the victim would have recoiled away from them and the attacker; and number two, they would have had a job even penetrating his clothes and body, as shear blades are sharp but not the ends of the blades – just quite blunt in fact. This man was not stabbed by the shears being used as a weapon.'

'So what do you think happened?'

'My professional opinion, and one I will prove in court if necessary...'

'It won't be.'

Latin looked disappointed at that. 'My professional opinion is that the victim impaled himself on the shears. I would suggest that the other person was using the shears and turned to face the victim, who was running towards him at the very moment the victim reached him whilst still holding the shears at chest level. The victim ran onto the shears, that's the only way enough force could have been exerted on the closed blades for them to penetrate the victims clothing, his rib cage and heart in one movement. He ran onto them, Justin – impaled himself. It was an accident; a rather nasty and fatal one, but an accident, not a deliberate murder.' Latin stood back a step from the body and crossed his arms like a lawyer in court having just given his closing statement and now defying anybody to doubt him.

'You seem sure of that?'

'I am, very sure.'

'Good. I'm quite glad, because both my Sergeant and I are of the opinion that the suspect for the person holding the shears isn't the type to deliberately use them as a weapon.'

****

Palmer returned to the Team Room. Gheeta gave him the news that the prints on the shears were indeed Riley's.

'He's not stupid is he, guv? Let's face it, if he went looking for Bloom with the shears as a weapon he would have had the sense to put gloves on – there's enough pairs laying around in a garden centre.'

'Latin thinks it was an accident.'

He explained Latin's premise to Gheeta and Claire.

'Sounds a reasonable explanation,' said Gheeta.

'Right then, let's recap what's happening.' Palmer counted off on his fingers. 'We've an arrest warrant out on Riley, FLOs are either with or on their way to Janet Bloom with the news and will stay with her for the night at least, forensics have the Watford scene tied up, and we have closed that garden centre and the Hanley's Garden Centre.'

'Short press release going out now,' added Gheeta.

'Good, and have we a uniform at Riley's bedsit?'

'Yes, all secured guv, and the local force are sealing off the Blooms' house, the Bloom stand at Chelsea has been isolated and screened off and forensics are there. I asked them to brush the sign on the Midnight Glory rose ASAP.'

'Any prizes for guessing whose prints are going to show up on that?'

'No.'

Claire added, 'I've asked for the CCTV from all the cameras at the showground for today to be sent to us.'

Palmer thought for a moment. 'Claire, check if there are any cameras focused on the road outside the showground; if there are we might get a shot of Riley arriving there. With a bit of luck he got there by cab and we can ANPR it backwards and see where he's coming from – maybe even an address he's using. And that's about it, unless you two can think of anything we've missed?'

'I think you should pop along to the Palace guv and get a statement from HRH.'

Palmer laughed. 'Probably the most exciting time she's ever had.'

'No, that would have been the time when she woke up and found that chap sitting on her bed,' said Claire.

'Chap?' said Palmer smiling. 'That wasn't a chap, it was Bateman hassling her for an MBE in the Honours list.'

They all laughed.

'Right then ladies, I think that will do for today. Home sweet home.'

'Steak and kidney pie, guv?'

Palmer smiled. 'Oh you know me so well, Sergeant. In fact it's toad in the hole with brown sauce tonight.'

****

Two things pleased Palmer when his squad car dropped him off at home: the drive was finished and looked good, and his car was parked on it complete with new wing mirror.

One thing that didn't please that much was the new wooden gate filling Benji's hole in the hedge. Oh well, can't win them all.

'Are you working on that Chelsea Flower Show shambles?' Mrs P. shouted from the kitchen as he hung up his coat and trilby and slipped on his slippers, after chasing Daisy round the hall five times before he managed to catch her and release them from her jaws.

'Yes, three murders and counting,' he replied as he went into the kitchen.

'Murders? Nothing about murders on the news, just that a black rose had been exhibited and somebody else has claimed it?'

'That somebody else who is claiming it is claiming it for a deceased rose breeder, and it seems the claim is right. That black rose might well be stolen property.'

'The Queen must have had a bit of a shock, by all accounts she was right in the middle of it.'

'She's all right, I popped in on my way home. She's had a couple of brandies and a fag to steady the nerves, she's fine – sends her regards and says can Daisy go and play with the corgis next week?'

Mrs P. ignored him and loudly put down a plate of toad in the hole in front of him before sitting opposite with her own plate. 'The drive's done, did you notice? And your car is back from the garage – didn't take long, did it?'

'They don't do repairs these days, just replacements. I bet that cost Benji a few quid.'

'You could offer to pay half.'

'What? Why?'

'You parked halfway across the entrance to his drive.'

'It's a double car drive, he still had a car and a half's width to drive through; and in any case if he hadn't ripped up our drive I wouldn't have had to park there in the first place.'

'Did you see the new gate?'

'Mmm,' Palmer mumbled through a mouthful of sausage.

'Looks nice, doesn't it.'

'I'll get a padlock.'

'You'll do no such thing, Justin Palmer. Anyway, I had a word with the chaps doing the drive and they're going to lay a similar herringbone brick path from the gate through the rose bed to the drive – look nice, won't it? Seven hundred.'

'Pounds?'

'Yes.'

Palmer laughed. 'Poor old Benji, does he know?'

'He's not paying for that, we are.'

'What?'

'He's paying for the gate.'

'I should hope so, he made the hole.'

'And one more surprise for you.'

'Go on.'

'You've just eaten two veggie sausages.'

****

TUESDAY

It was a plan that could go badly wrong. Riley showered, ate a good full English breakfast, paid his B & B bill and made his way by bus to Watford. He noted the police presence outside Bloom's Garden Centre and avoided walking past it by taking a detour round the back streets until he reached a leafy avenue where he could see the press and nosy members of the public outside the Blooms' detached Victorian house, being kept back behind crime scene tape stretched across the end of the drive manned by three uniformed officers. He knew the house well, especially the large en-suite bedroom where he had spent time with Janet when Edward was abroad buying and ordering stock for the centres. He walked past on the opposite side of the road and noted both Blooms' cars were in the drive; Janet must be home.

He walked on to the end of the street and turned right; sixty metres along that street an alleyway led off between the back gardens of the houses and a golf course – he knew it well as that alleyway had been his access and exit on his evenings with Janet. He peered along it; he couldn't see any people – the press obviously weren't aware of it or they'd have been all over it.

The large shrubs and trees that the residents had planted to stop stray golf balls from smashing their greenhouse windows gave him plenty of cover as he stealthily made his way to the back gate of the Blooms' garden. It was a steel bar gate so he could see through into the garden. All was quiet, a short path led from the gate through a shrubbery onto a lawn bordered on both sides by large shrubs planted for privacy from neighbours. From the far end of the lawn four wide flag stone steps led up onto a patio furnished with a large all-weather outside table and chairs. At the back of the patio the double French doors led off it into the back lounge; they were shut.

Riley let himself into the garden, releasing the padlock on the gate with the key that Janet had given him that he hadn't returned. He stooped down out of sight behind the plants and waited; there wasn't an officer posted at the patio, but maybe they made patrols every so often. He gave it ten minutes – no sign of anybody. Quickly he made his way to the patio, hugging the border for some cover. On the patio he stopped abruptly and ducked behind one of the chairs as one side of the

French doors opened outwards. He held his breath.

'I wondered how long it would be before you came.' Janet Bloom smiled as he rose slowly from behind the chair, waiting for a police officer to join her. None did. 'Lost your tongue, Jim? You'd better come in, unless you intend to murder me and run like you did Edward?' She held the door open invitingly and went inside. Jim followed.

****

Palmer didn't really like working weekends, especially not Sundays. On Sundays he liked to relax and watch the football on Sky. Barcelona were his favourite team, but they seemed to have lost their way this season and had management issues – as well as Sky losing the Serie A contract. So he had to make do with his boyhood favourites Arsenal, and they were on that afternoon, a London derby against Tottenham. He was going to miss it.

In the Team Room he checked with Gheeta on the state of play.

'Janet Bloom is at home. She was sedated overnight; didn't want any relatives to be called in to be with her and sent the FLO away this morning. I had a word with the FLO and she says Janet is not showing much grief and seems in complete control of her emotions. The local uniform branch are at the house, as are the press and media. Did you see the papers this morning?'

'No, I don't bother – it's yesterday's news usually. I bet they had a feast with the Chelsea thing.'

'They did – depending on which paper you read that black rose is worth anything from a hundred grand to ten million.'

Palmer laughed. 'Anything on Riley?'

'No guv, no sign. Shall I put a mugshot out to the media?'

'No, not yet. Get a plainclothes officer to keep Alison Burnley company at home, nice and quietly, then all the places he might go are covered.'

****

'Sit down.' Janet Bloom pointed to an armchair in her lounge as she sat in one herself; between them an occasional table made a barrier. She showed Jim a key fob in her hand. 'See this, Jim? It's a panic alarm. Try anything and I press it and the house alarm goes off like an air-raid warning. I take it you've seen the police at the front?'

Jim nodded.

'Was it worth it Jim, was it really worth it? You're going to prison for most of the rest of your life. For what – for that?' She pointed to a sideboard behind Jim alongside the French doors that he hadn't noticed on the way in. On top of the sideboard the black rose mother plant stood, complete and in bloom. 'Lovely isn't it, Jim? And it's mine now, so you failed – killed Edward for nothing.'

'I didn't kill Edward, it was an accident.'

She laughed. 'Must have been some amazing accident for a pair of shears to plunge into his body up to the hilt. The police are after you for murder, Jim.'

'They know about Angela Robinson and Charlie Hilton – they know you killed them,' he bluffed, putting pressure on her hoping to make her act out the final part of his plan. 'Burnley told them.'

'Me? Not me, Jim. I didn't kill them, I'm in the clear. If they do get proof on any murders it will be against Edward – I knew nothing about it.'

'Alison Burnley is talking.'

Janet laughed. 'Poor Alison, who do you think the police will believe: me, or a bent bookkeeper who embezzled thousands from her employers?'

'I should have realised what sort of person you were at college. What did you do with the Vice Principal after you got your Degree? Dropped him like a stone I bet.'

'You'd win the bet, Jim. Men are so stupid and vain, especially the older ones. You think I married Edward for love? Don't be stupid, I married for money and all the trappings that brings. Love doesn't make the world go round, Jim – money does, and now I've got lots of it, and with the black rose much more than I ever imagined. So in a way I suppose I should be thanking you.' She paused for a moment. 'But I'm not. I'm going to press this button when we've finished.'

'Press it now, we've finished.' Jim was getting worried his plan might falter. Had he misjudged her after all?

'No we haven't, Jim. I intend to savour this moment – in fact I was going to open a bottle of champagne for us to toast my future with you, but then I remembered you don't drink – no fun toasting something on your own, so when I saw you hiding in the garden I put the kettle on for a cup of tea. Care to join me in a toast with tea? The water's boiled, probably be the last decent cup you'll ever have. I don't think prison tea can be much good.' She stood and made her way to the door, holding the fob between her fingers threateningly. 'Don't move. One move and I press this.'

Jim didn't intend to move; a slight smile turned the corners of his lips. It now looked like the plan was working – he hadn't misjudged her. Janet was back in no time with two cups of tea and a plate of biscuits. She put them down on the table in between them. 'Enjoy it, Jim.' She took a sip from her cup as Jim pretended to do the same and screwed his face up.

'Urgh, no sugar.'

'You don't take sugar, I remembered that from college. You don't take sugar.'

'I do now, I have type 2 diabetes. I can't drink that without sugar.'

'Okay, I'll get some.'

Janet left the room and Jim swapped the cups quickly. She returned with a sugar bowl and spoon.

'Here.'

He scooped a spoon into the cup and took a gulp. 'That's better. Bit of a funny taste – your milk off?' He drank more. Then he sat still and started to cough; the cough turned into a rasping and a struggle for breath. He slumped forward, trying to speak.

Janet Bloom laughed. 'Did you really think I'd let you go to the police, Jim? Did you really think I'd take the chance that they might believe just one little piece of your story and start to investigate – turn up our bank statements, take another look at Robinson and Hilton's deaths? Don't be silly Jim, no way was that going to happen. You've drunk tea with aconite, just like the Hanleys and poor old Mr Hilton. You've got about two minutes, Jim. Take a good look at the rose, Jim. Was it worth dying for?' She raised her cup in a toast. 'To the black rose, and the owner of it: me.' She drank some of the tea and offered another toast. 'To Jim Riley, the nearly man.' She emptied her cup. Jim stopped the rasping and sat up straight, looking Janet straight in the eye across the low table and his face broke into a smile. She showed surprise at first before looking at her cup and dropping it from her hand.

'You bastard, you guessed.' Her voice rasped the words out.

'Oh yes, I guessed. The only reason I came here today was to tempt you into poisoning me and you fell for it. Not all men are as stupid as you think.'

Janet Bloom was struggling for breath. The fob fell from her hand as she lurched forward onto the low table, her head sideways, eyes wide open. She tried but couldn't speak.

'Look at the rose, Janet – it's the last thing you'll see. Now you tell me, was it worth it?'

Her body slumped lifeless onto the table and the weight pulled it over as she slid off it onto the carpet.

Jim picked up his teacup. He checked the hall: empty. He could see the shadow of a policeman outside the front door; he made his way stealthily to it and slipped the catch on and quietly slid a bolt across that was beneath the lock – obviously the Blooms had been very protective of their property. He quickly made his way back down the hall and into the kitchen, washed and dried the cup and saucer and put it away in the cupboard with the rest of the set. He took a tea towel off the side and back in the lounge wiped down the table and the French door handles just in case he'd touched them. Picking up the key fob from where it had fallen on the floor he put it in his pocket, and then gathering the rose from the sideboard and draping the towel over it he went out to the patio, closing the door with his elbow, careful not to touch anything. He made his way to the rear garden gate and slipped through, closing the padlock on it. He stood still and silent for a few moments before taking out the fob and pressing the button.

Janet had been right – all hell broke loose. The decibel wailing of the alarm must have created havoc at the front of the house. Jim hurried along the alleyway to the street, throwing the fob and back gate key into an overgrown patch of nettles and weeds on the back of the golf course. He turned into the street at the end of the alley and at the Blooms' avenue he stopped and looked along to their house, where press, media and public were trying to work out what was happening; as the alarm screamed in the background, more neighbours were coming quickly from their houses and joining the clamour. He took the other way and quickened his pace.

Jim walked, and kept walking. He hadn't any more plan, it was over. He laughed as the tension left him – it was over, it had worked. He had taken a chance that Janet would try to kill him to keep her story running and it had worked; he guessed that if he had taken the poison she would probably have said he had the poison and tried to poison her but she saw it and swapped the cups. She would have said it must have been Jim who poisoned the others. She would have said... well, it didn't matter now what she would have said, because she isn't going to say anything now, is she?

After a while he collected his thoughts. What about the rose? He didn't want it, he wished he'd never seen it – he wished Hanley had never bred it. It needed to go and go for good. He looked around and spied a row of black wheelie bins lined up against a wall at the back of the pavement waiting for the refuse lorry; some were overfull and their lids propped open by too many bin bags of rubbish squashed inside, so the collection was due. He went to the ones that had lids shut and looked inside; the first two were full to the brim, the third was three quarters full only. He dropped the rose and the towel inside and shut the lid. Job done.

****

Palmer's squad car arrived at the front of the Blooms' house and drew up on the other side of the road behind an ambulance, three other police cars and a forensic Transit.

Gheeta pointed to it. 'Reg Frome's here already, guv.'

The crowd had quadrupled, mostly media, press and paparazzi. They recognised Palmer as soon as he got out of the car; he'd been hoping to surprise them and duck under the crime scene tape and inside before that happened. No chance; he was surrounded.

'What's going on, Mr Palmer?'

'Is Janet Bloom inside?

'Is Janet Bloom dead?'

'Has there been a murder, Mr Palmer?'

'Is the black rose inside?'

'Has it been stolen?

He caught sight of DS Singh slipping under the tape unchallenged as two officers pushed a way for him through the throng and under the tape.

'What it is to be a celebrity, eh guv?' she said when he joined her on the drive. 'How many autographs did you sign?'

Palmer dismissed the comment with a cold look and they crunched their way to the front door, which was splintered in two with one half on the ground and the other hanging from a brass hinge.

'What happened there?' he asked the officer standing guard.

'We couldn't get in, sir. The lady's panic alarm went off and she'd locked and bolted the door from the inside. We had to break it down.'

'No door round the back? asked Gheeta.

'There is a double French door.'

'Did you try those?'

'No.'

Gheeta raised her eyebrows at the officer in disbelief.

Palmer didn't want to get involved in an inquest as to what, why and who over the doors. 'Come on, let's take a look.'

A box of overshoes lay open by the door; forensics were making sure that anybody entering wouldn't contaminate the crime scene. They both put a pair on, Gheeta turned her laptop on and recorded the scene as they entered.

'Mind where you put your clumsy feet.' Reg Frome in a full white paper forensic suit, overshoes, gloves, mask and hat beckoned them from the lounge door.

'You got here quickly, Reg?' Palmer was surprised.

'Not really. Having done the forensics on Edward Bloom at Watford and at the Chelsea showground yesterday we are listed in comms as the forensic team handling the Bloom case so I got the call. She's dead, did comms tell you?'

'No.' Palmer was a bit taken aback. 'Just that there had been a serious incident at the Blooms' house, no details.'

Frome beckoned them both into the lounge where forensic plates were in place around a black body bag and a snapper was photographing the scene from all angles.

Palmer nodded toward it. 'Janet Bloom?'

'Yes, let me fill you in. When we arrived Janet Bloom was on her back on the carpet with the ambulance crew trying to revive her; they had taken over from the first responders who had tried for twenty minutes until the ambulance arrived and took over with all their paraphernalia, but no good – she was dead. Nobody else in the house, no sign of a break in and no weapon; no wounds are visible but pathology will have to make sure about that – not our department – but bearing in mind cause of death to the Hanleys, I wouldn't be surprised if it was poison. In fact it probably was, as we've found a small bottle of white powder in the kitchen cabinet that I'll get analysed as soon as we get back to the lab.'

'It's going to be aconite,' Palmer stated.

'Could be.'

'Suicide then?'

'Well, only one empty cup and saucer here on the floor where they had fallen when she fell and upset the table, plus biscuits and a plate. One cup does indicate it may be suicide.'

'That's hard to believe of Janet Bloom, guv,' said Gheeta.

'Yes, it is.'

'If she has been poisoned somebody else could have put the poison into her cup before she drank it.'

Frome shrugged. 'No forensic signs so far of anybody else being here.'

'I thought she had an FLO with her?' said Gheeta.

'Apparently Mrs Bloom sent her away. Her personal doctor came in at eight thirty and checked her over; she seemed fine, good state of mind, so he prescribed some antidepressants to be taken if she felt she needed them and she sent the FLO away at nine o'clock.'

'Okay.' Palmer left the lounge and peered into the kitchen. Something caught his eye, but he was interrupted by a uniformed DI coming up the hall.

'Detective Superintendent Palmer?' said the uniform.

'Detective *Chief* Superintendent Palmer actually,' replied Palmer. It had taken forty odd years in the force to get that title and he was justly proud of it.

'Apologies sir,' said the uniform. 'I'm DI Salcombe, local station – I've been allocated OIC on this crime scene. Day off and being short of officers I was called from home so not up to speed yet.'

'Day off? How do you get a day off if you're short of officers?' He waved his own question away. 'Never mind. This is my sergeant DS Singh, she will bring you up to speed and then I'll have a word, okay?'

'Yes, sir.'

Gheeta moved out to the patio and took Salcombe through the events. Palmer went back into the kitchen where the snapper had started to work.

'Make sure I get a full set of photos won't you.'

'Yes sir, will do. I'll have them ready for the morning.'

'Quicker than Boots then,' Palmer joked.

The snapper gave a false smile; he must have heard that remark a thousand times.

Palmer wandered through the lounge and checked the evidence bags forensics were accumulating: fibres and hairs from the carpet and chairs, fingertip strips and DNA scrapes from anywhere a human might rest their hands or head. What he was looking for was missing. He stepped out to the patio where Gheeta had just finished with Salcombe who had made numerous notes.

'There's a golf course at the end of the garden, sir,' said Gheeta.

'Handy if you play golf. You play, Salcombe?'

'No, sir.'

'Me neither.'

'And there's an alleyway between it and the houses,' Gheeta finished her sentence.

Palmer took notice. 'With a back gate?' he asked Salcombe.

'Yes sir, they all have back gates.'

Palmer didn't need telling twice. 'Right, get that alleyway sealed off from any entrances to it. Tell DCS Frome about the gate – don't let anybody near it until he says so, and then I want a fingertip search along the whole length of that alley and its edges. If there was somebody other than Mrs Bloom in the house they certainly didn't leave by the front, and I'm pretty sure that there was another person.'

Gheeta raised her eyebrows. 'You are?'

'Yes, the officer on the door said the alarm was activated by, and I quote *the lady's personal alarm* – that's a fob, and there's no fob in the evidence bags.'

Gheeta could see the reasoning. 'So if Janet Bloom didn't press it who did, and why?'

'I don't think she pressed it, I think there was another person and it's beginning to look more and more likely. I think he or she poisoned Janet Bloom and went out the back way, setting off the alarm to cause panic once he or she was down that alley and away.'

'If there was another person.'

'Yes, but if there wasn't then where's the fob? It can't disappear into thin air.'

Salcombe looked worried. 'My chief isn't going to be too happy to lose men on a fingertip search. We're short as it is and he's always moaning.'

Palmer bristled; he hated negative observations. If things had to be done you got on and did them.

'In that case I'll have Assistant Commissioner Bateman give him a call first thing and kick his arse, DI Salcombe.'

Salcombe smile. 'I'd appreciate that, sir.'

'Consider it done.'

****

Palmer walked slowly round Dulwich Park in the evening sunlight, which was growing stronger as each day of May passed. Daisy wandered in and out of the bushes in the vain hope of a squirrel to chase or a dropped dog biscuit to eat; no luck on either so far. He was so engrossed in his thoughts about the case that several *hellos* and *evening Justin* from neighbours passing with their dogs went unanswered.

It was a strange set of affairs. The Blooms were nasty people, or had been nasty people when alive; the whole case was centred on them murdering for gain, but the two people who were probably going to jail were basically innocent workers who had been dragged into it by the Blooms' avarice, their promises and their threats. Sometimes the law doesn't take enough account of mitigating circumstances. All right, both Riley and Burnley were guilty of misdemeanours and their futures would be blighted by them; but the real culprits had paid the price, and Burnley and Riley were collateral damage. He'd seen it many times before in his career, otherwise decent people being forced by intimidation, threats and fear into criminal acts they wouldn't dream of doing under usual circumstances. Weak people were the bread and butter of the criminal classes – always have been, probably always will be. If Riley and Burnley went to prison Burnley would probably be bullied to death, and Riley most likely come out a paid-up member of the criminal class. Palmer really didn't want to see them go down that road.

He sighed loudly.

'Come on Daisy, home time.'

****

WEDNESDAY

AC Bateman was only too glad to pull rank on the local officers at Watford and insist on an immediate fingertip search of the back alley, as he was already taking flack from the Home Office about the case; they in turn were taking flack from the Home Secretary, whose government had been elected on a 'tough on crime' agenda. But then all political parties shout that before elections, but truth be known they can't do anything about crime without tackling the basic reasons why people commit crimes, which is the widening gap between those who have and those who have not, with those who have not wanting to join those who have.

'What time is Alison Burnley coming in?' Palmer asked Gheeta as he returned to the Team Room to find DS Atkins there with Gheeta and Claire.

'DS Atkins has found a rather nice little scam in the Hanley accounts, guv. You'll love it,' said Gheeta.

Palmer sat down. 'Go on Atkins, what is it now?'

'Well sir...' Atkins sat and referred to his notes. 'There were a series of cheques for substantial amounts going out of the Hanley account in the six weeks prior to the eighty thousand pounds being paid in to it, and these cheques were all paid into the Bloom's Garden Centre account; although looking at the actual cheques returned to the bank they were actually made out to Bloom's, although in the accounts book the bookkeeper has listed them as being to various different suppliers.'

Palmer leant forward. 'Go on.'

'These cheques totalled eighty thousand pounds, and they sent Hanley into overdrawn status on his account to that amount.'

Palmer sat up and thought for a moment. 'Brilliant, bloody brilliant – what a scam… Bloom and Burnley working together send Hanley eighty grand into the red, and then step in and help him out, using his own money.'

Atkins nodded. 'Yes.'

'Bloody brilliant. What time is Burnley coming in?' he asked Gheeta.

'Ten o'clock, guv.'

'Right, take her through the results of her embezzlements that DS Atkins has listed. Over the years he reckons she's had about forty thousand pounds for herself off Robinson, Hilton and Hanley. It didn't go into her normal bank account either, it went into an Isle of Man account and the majority is still there. Atkins, you make a call and get a freeze on that account and then when we interview Burnley we can remind her of the Proceeds of Crime Act, which means she could lose that money and her house if the court insist on her paying it back in total plus interest. And this is important, Sergeant,' he said to Gheeta. 'Don't charge her. Tell her that we are still making enquiries and further charges relating to her being an accomplice to murder may follow. Frighten the silly woman and put her into a remand cell to think about it, and then get the duty solicitor in and have her write a signed statement. I'll want to talk to her maybe later today or tomorrow.'

'You think she'll cough up the money in return for a lenient sentence?'

'I think she will, she would be stupid not to. Forty grand or whatever is left of it won't be worth much when she comes out in twenty years' time – remind her of that. Any news on Jim Riley?'

'No, none. He's disappeared.'

The internal wall phone rang and Claire answered it. She listened and told the caller to hold on.

'He hasn't disappeared, sir. Jim Riley is in reception asking for you.'

Palmer and Gheeta looked at each other, wondering what Riley was playing at. Palmer broke the silence. 'Sergeant, go and take him to the custody suite – charge him with the theft of valuable plants from Hanley's Garden Centre, just a basic charge, and put him in a remand cell too. Not the same one as Burnley. Then when you finish putting the frighteners on Burnley do the same to Riley, tell him accomplice to murder charges may follow. Get a signed statement. Well, that's a turn up for the books.'

Gheeta smiled. 'We could have this case done and dusted today, guv. Do you want me to have a word with the CPS later and see if they'd be prepared to charge the pair with the evidence we've got?'

'That's being a bit optimistic, Sergeant – no, not yet. Right, you take care of Burnley and Riley, I've got a couple of people to go and see.'

Both Claire and Gheeta looked at him quizzically.

'Who?' asked Gheeta.

'Never you mind, I have a plan.' He gave them a smile with raised eyebrows.

'I hope it's a good plan guv, not a Baldrick type plan?'

'Wait and see.'

****

'It could work.' Michael Whitley of Whitley Solicitors rubbed his chin thoughtfully. 'It would certainly seem an ideal way of getting closure to the case. I was talking to my father after your last visit, Chief Superintendent, and he knows Riley quite well; he was shocked at the Hanleys' deaths and equally shocked at the thought that Riley was involved. But now we know the full story and how the Blooms manipulated him, I'm sure what you suggest is a good move; no creditors have come forward with any claim on the estate so we can go forward with your suggestion. I'll draw up the necessary paperwork and clear it with HMRC once you get the Hanleys' bank to agree and get our insolvency chaps to start the ball rolling.'

Palmer stood up from the very comfortable chair in Whitley's office and they shook hands.

'I'll give you a call once I've seen the bank.' Palmer stood to leave. 'Oh, one more thing – have you a card?'

'Yes, yes of course.' Whitley took one from a desk drawer and passed it over. 'Have you ever thought of swapping your side of the law to our side, Chief Superintendent? I think you might be very good at it.'

They both laughed.

****

'I thought the lady in reception was pulling my leg, but obviously she wasn't.'

Palmer was in the HSBC bank at Watford with the Hanleys' business banker. The sign on his desk gave his name as Lloyd Barclay.

Lloyd Barclay smiled; he'd lost count of the times in his career that customers had questioned his name. He was really fed up with explaining it too, but always had to.

'My dad was a banker and so were my three uncles and my grandfather. I think they took a lot of stick in the banking world for having the surname Barclay and decided to take out their irritation on me. But to be honest, Chief Inspector, I don't think it's done me any harm – not likely to forget me, are you?'

Palmer laughed. 'That's true.'

'Would you like a tea or coffee before you bring me up to date with the Hanleys' affairs? Obviously we have everything on stop at present until the situation becomes clear.'

Palmer declined. 'Well, it is all fairly clear now. I think the best thing is for me to take you through the case from the beginning and then get your reaction to a suggestion to save the business and the staff's jobs. I've already spoken to the company solicitor and he's quite happy to give it a try.'

'Sounds good. Hanley had a good business overall – a few blips now and again but only one that gave us concern, and then that seemed to be settled pretty quickly. Go on Chief Superintendent, I'm all ears.'

After a long explanation of the case, the Blooms, Riley and Burnley's involvement and a way Palmer could see an outcome that satisfied all involved, Lloyd Barclay smiled.

'Ever thought of swapping the law for banking, Chief Superintendent? I think you'd be rather good at it. Yes, I can't see any objection to your idea. I'll get some paperwork sorted out to start the ball rolling.'

'Do you have a card I might have?'

'Of course.' Lloyd Barclay took one from a desk drawer and passed it over.

****

THURSDAY

'I think you've gone soft in the head, guv.' Gheeta was looking very surprised. 'I hope it works, but if it all goes belly up they'll blame you.'

'I think it's a great idea sir,' countered Claire. 'With the checks and balances you've put in place it can't go wrong.'

Palmer had spent the morning dotting the i's and crossing the t's of his plan in the peace and solitude of his cramped office across the corridor from the Team Room, and when he was satisfied all was in order and got the okay on the phone from Michael Whitley he told Gheeta and Claire what he had in mind.

Gheeta passed him a small evidence bag. 'By the way, Reg Frome sent this over earlier. It's what you expected, Riley's print as well.'

Palmer put it on the bench in front of him next to a set of the photos from Janet Bloom's house the snapper had sent over.

There was a knock on the door and the custody officer walked in followed by Riley, Burnley and two officers.

'The two prisoners you asked to be brought up sir,' the officer spoke.

'Ah, good, thank you George. Leave them with us, they'll be fine.'

'You sure, sir? I can leave one of my chaps if you like?'

'No, no, we'll be fine.'

'All right sir, sign here please.'

Palmer signed the prisoner transfer form and the custody officers left.

Riley and Burnley stood like two miscreant children called to the headmaster's office.

Palmer smiled at them. 'Sit down, you two. We are going to have a chat.'

He indicated two chairs the other side of the bench and waited whilst they sat down. 'Right, I am aware that neither of you are actual murderers, but a very good case can be put in court to have you charged with being accomplices to murder. My own view is that you were both a bit stupid and saw a way to riches without much work involved. What neither of you knew was who the people you were dealing with were, the people who held out the chance of money and status – in other words, the Blooms. Edward Bloom, a career criminal who probably murdered Angela Robinson, and together with his wife Janet Bloom probably poisoned Charlie Hilton, and definitely poisoned the Hanleys. I think you, Aliso , suspected them of having a hand in four deaths.' He stopped and looked at Burnley, who remained stock still.

'Yes.' Her voice was very faint. 'I had my suspicions.'

'But you couldn't voice them, could you Alison? Because you'd had your fingers in the till and Bloom knew it. A word from him and you'd be in court – career finished and a criminal record.'

Burnley hung her head a little as Palmer nodded and carried on. 'And you, Jim. You knew they killed the Hanleys, they would have told you and told you that they would implicate you in the killings if you told anybody, by virtue of you having stolen the black rose for them.'

Riley didn't move or speak.

'So you both came to be in the same situation; a relatively minor theft had led you both into a position where the Blooms had you over a barrel. If they were arrested and charged with murder, they could implicate you two and you would be charged with murder or as accomplices in murder.' He sat back and let that sink in. 'I don't believe either of you were involved directly in any murders or implicated in them. As bookkeeper, Alison, you had the open opportunity to embezzle because your employers trusted you too much, and you took that opportunity. As general manager, Jim, you could take roses out of the Hanley Garden Centre without anybody being suspicious; you kept Bloom up to date on the progress of the black rose as Janet lavished her attention on you, rekindling the old urges from your college days. You fell for it Jim – *femme fatale*.

'And when the black rose was just about ready for commercial exploitation, Edward Bloom came to you Alison, didn't he?' Burnley froze. 'He came to you and reminded you that he knew all about the money you were stealing; it wasn't great amounts, a couple of hundred a month, but it would get you sacked and your career ended if he told Geoff Hanley. But he offered a way out for you: steal a larger amount over a couple of months with the fake invoice system you used, an amount of eighty thousand pounds, and he would remain silent. You did it, didn't you Alison?' Palmer waited for an answer; there wasn't one, but an affirmative nod of Burnley's head. Palmer continued.

'And the money didn't go into your Isle of Man account, did it?' Burnley's head rose sharply. 'Oh yes Alison, we know all about that account. No, it didn't go there, it went into the Bloom's account, and on Bloom's instructions you told Geoff Hanley that he had spent too much and was overdrawn past his limit, and no doubt he had a great shock when you told him just how much past his limit. But help was at hand; you told him you worked for another garden centre who was looking to expand, Bloom's, maybe they would help? And help they did – they gave Geoff Hanley eighty thousand pounds of his own stolen money for a half share in the business and a way out of debt; debt that you told people was due to his gambling. You told me that too, but Geoff Hanley never gambled in his life.'

Burnley broke down and slumped sobbing with her head in her hands. Palmer ignored it. 'But the partnership never materialised. The money went through, but no book work or legal documents were ever drawn up by Mr Hanley's solicitor, because Mr Hanley never instructed him to do so. I wonder why? You'd think Mr Hanley would be so grateful for being helped out of a financial hole by Bloom that it would all go ahead. But it didn't. Why? Was Geoff Hanley a bit suspicious? Maybe he cottoned onto what had happened? Bloom's character was well known in the British Association of Rose Breeders – they even banned him, so word might have got round and Hanley smelt a rat? Perhaps he checked your account book and saw that the money from the cheques that were made out to various suppliers all ended up in one account, the Blooms'; perhaps he played the Blooms, perhaps he let them give him his own money back, knowing all the time it was his, and never intended to take Bloom on as a partner? We will never know, but whatever happened the partnership didn't go through and that drew the anger of the Blooms and the murder of the Hanleys. All over a rose – a very special rose.'

Palmer turned to Riley. 'And all this time, Jim, you were unaware that your actions with the black rose had brought about two murders. You didn't know what was happening until my Sergeant and I paid our first visit to you; I can tell when people are genuinely shocked by news, and you were genuinely shock by the news of the Hanleys' deaths. I'm thinking that you are an intelligent man, Jim, and it wouldn't have taken you long to piece things together; you knew the partnership was agreed, you probably didn't know about the eighty thousand pound scam but it didn't matter; as far as you knew everything was going to plan, the partnership was going through and that would negate your theft of the black rose as Bloom would then own half of it.

'But now with Hanley's death there was a problem. You knew something had gone wrong and Bloom had killed them; I bet that first meeting you had with the Blooms after we told you about the Hanleys' deaths was pretty explosive. No doubt they told you the partnership had not gone through, or maybe they said it had before the Hanley's deaths, so they were outright owners of the black rose now. You realised Janet Bloom had played you, they both had, and they had backed you into a corner like they had backed Alison into a corner. You had stolen a very expensive plant and double crossed your employer. Was it then that you decided to take revenge? Probably, but what kind of revenge? You couldn't kill the Blooms, that would be stupid – but you could stop them getting their hands on Geoff Hanley's black rose. You could tell the world about their scheme and out them for theft and murder. But how? Well, first you had to destroy the stock, and that's when Edward Bloom was killed...'

Riley interrupted. 'I didn't murder him, it was an accident.'

Palmer smiled. 'I didn't say you murdered him, Jim. I said he was killed. I know you didn't murder him – the pathologist will testify to that if need be. You couldn't possibly stab a pair of shears through his clothes and up to the handles into his body, not unless you're Superman, and you're not. The pathologist thinks he ran onto the shears whilst you held them. I think you were in the greenhouse destroying the black rose cuttings as part of your revenge and Bloom found you there and ran at you; you turned with the shears in your hand and he impaled himself on them, am I right?'

Riley nodded.

'I thought so. And then there was the Chelsea Show and the big reveal of the black rose on the Bloom stand – what an ideal place and time to let the world know the Blooms murdered the Hanleys. I have to say Jim, it was a brilliant idea, and it worked; I'd been trying to keep a low profile on the case until I had concrete evidence to arrest the Blooms with, and with one piece of paper you blew that away and had the press up in arms, and the black rose was the only story in town. That only left Janet Bloom – how could you get rid of her? You knew she would want to kill you; after all she would be thinking you had killed Edward. She knew we were looking for you and if you talked and told us about the poisoning of the Hanleys, her world would tumble down. We already knew about the poison Jim – we knew from the beginning, but we needed the proof. She guessed you'd pay her a visit and you intended to. You intended to let her have a go at poisoning you, but you would be prepared for that move, and you saw it as a way to complete your revenge. So you did pay her a visit.'

Jim Riley opened his mouth to speak but Palmer waved a silencing hand.

'Don't deny it Jim, you were there. You knew the house and you knew the back entrance; after all, you'd used it to visit Janet Bloom when Edward was away after she had rekindled your relationship. Oh yes, you were there; you went in the back way along the alley and sat with her in the lounge, knowing she'd try to kill you. How would she do it? You had taken a chance on poison, a chance that paid off – she did indeed try to poison you with a cup of tea. What did you do Jim, somehow swap the cups so she drank the poison she'd prepared for you? You did a good job tidying up afterwards, just leaving the one cup, the one with poison residue in it; you thought it would look like Janet Bloom was shattered with grief after the death of Edward and had taken her own life, taken her own life with the poison they had killed the

Hanleys with, thus pointing the finger firmly at the Blooms as the killers. Very clever Jim, but not clever enough.'

Palmer pushed a photo of the kitchen across to Riley. 'Take a close look, Jim. See the side of the sink? Two used tea bags – *two*, Jim, not one, Janet Bloom made two cups of tea, so who was there with her? Only one person it could be: you. You knew the back way, and nobody had come in the front as the local uniform boys had been there all night and day. One other thing, Jim, you didn't think it through. You set the alarm off on purpose as you left – the panel indicated it had been activated by a personal fob – but there was no fob near Janet's body or anywhere in the house. You didn't think of that, did you Jim? Everything had gone to plan, the poison, the cup swap, the clean-up and the escape through the back gate – but two tea bags and no fob were mistakes.' Palmer took the small evidence bag sent from Reg Frome and tipped out the key fob and back gate key. 'We found them Jim, fingertip search of the alleyway – and guess whose print is on the fob button.'

Palmer sat back and took a deep breath. 'So, there we have it – two silly people getting involved in things they can't control and becoming sucked into a world of murder beyond their control.' He lightened up and smiled. 'But let's face it, neither of you are bad people at heart and I'm sure that the charges of theft, which are the charges that will be put to you by the Crown Prosecution Service in the County Court, will carry suspended sentences if my office were to have a chat with the judge at a pre-trial hearing.'

Both Burnley and Riley looked up with hope flashing across their faces. Gheeta and Claire exchanged mystified glances. What was Palmer up to?

Palmer held up a hand to diminish their raised hopes. 'I said *if my office were to have a chat with the Judge – if,* and that *if* depends on you two agreeing to a deal. And this is the deal. Have you heard of a pre-pack administration?'

Both Burnley and Riley hadn't.

'Okay, let me explain. A pre-packaged administration is when a company goes into administration and the solicitors handling that administration have already sorted out who the new owners will be and what they will pay; it's a way a company can continuing trading without a break in receipts and also loses its debts. Hanley's Garden Centre has been put into one such deal and will be bought out of it by you two.'

A shocked silence was broken by Riley. 'How? It can't be, I haven't any money to buy it with.'

'No, but Alison has, haven't you Alison? Alison has a quantity of cash that actually belongs to Mr Hanley, Angela Robinson and Charlie Hilton – thirty two thousand pounds to be precise, all now frozen in an Isle of Man account. Ten thousand of that will buy the Hanley's Garden Centre out of administration and twenty thousand will go into a company trading bank account with two thousand in the safe for current use as things are set up. Bearing in mind Alison's past financial actions with company accounts, the bank will be monitoring the account closely and quarterly meetings will be arranged with the business banker allocated to the account.' He addressed Burnley. 'If that money doesn't go into the company account then a Proceeds of Crime order will whisk it away into the coffers of HMRC. I know which option I'd take.' He turned to Riley. 'You, Jim, will be general manager and all company cheques will need to be signed by both of you, who will be equal partners in the company. I have one proviso for you, Jim – you don't do any rose breeding. Agreed?'

Riley nodded. 'Agreed.'

Palmer looked from one to another of them. 'You will both go to court, but as I said before, whatever sentence you get will be suspended and you'll be free to get on and make something with your lives. Bear in mind that no agreement to this plan will undoubtedly result in you both going to prison, while an agreement will get you both suspended sentences and you keep your freedom as long as you behave yourselves. So, that's the deal. If you want a little time to consider it between yourselves you can use my office?' He sat back.

Riley looked at Burnley and they both stuttered into laughter brought on by relief.

Palmer laughed too. 'Okay, I think I've got your answer. Here.' He passed two business cards across the table. 'They are your company solicitors and bank. First thing tomorrow you go to the solicitor and sign the pre-pack agreement, then you go to the bank and have them organise a transfer of the Isle of Man money into your new business account and give specimen signatures. I'll have our forensic accountant unfreeze the Isle of Man account in the morning. Don't forget that ten thousand of that will be going to buy the business. Now, I really don't want to see you again until your County Court appearance; your solicitor will guide you through that as well. I suggest you compose yourselves and take a cab over to Hanley's and ring round the staff and tell them they still have their jobs, who the new owners are, and get them back to work. Then you'd better get selling lots plants and compost bags – solicitors and bankers don't come cheap. I'll get the uniform officers and the crime tape removed by the morning. Off you go, and make it work.'

Palmer stood and indicated the door. Riley and Burnley were gushing in their thanks, and when Burnley gave Palmer a hug Gheeta stepped in before all the air was crushed out of him and ushered them out of the door, down the corridor and into the lift. She came back into the Team Room and gave Palmer a big smile and a quizzical look.

'So Chief Superintendent Palmer of the Yard has turned into Saint Justin of Yard then, has he?'

'If I can't persuade the judge to give suspended sentences I'll be Saint Cock-up of the Yard.'

****

Dorothy Randall was just about to take the first sip of her regular mid-morning cup of coffee sitting in the front room of her one-bed pensioner's sheltered accommodation bungalow on a small social housing complex off the Rickmansworth Road out of Watford when she saw the caretaker Harry Cribbs coming up the small path to her front door. She put her coffee down and opened it before he could knock.

'Hello Harry, what do you want?' she said as she opened it. Harry stood there holding what looked like a battered pot plant in his hands. 'Bought me a present, have you?'

'No.' Harry wasn't in a good mood; looking after twenty pensioners in their sheltered accommodation bungalows sometimes sent his stress levels through the roof. 'Mrs Randall, you know the rules about the wheelie bins – black for household rubbish and green for garden.'

'Yes, I know that.'

'So why did you put this in your black bin then? The bin men weren't very happy.'

'I didn't. What is it?'

'An old rose bush. Here.' He held it out to Dorothy. 'You can have it back and put it in your green bin.'

'It's not mine Harry, I didn't put it in the bin – must have been some passerby getting rid of it, not me. Quite pretty though, isn't it? Dark flowers, attractive.'

'You think so?'

'Yes. Leave it with me, I'll trim off the broken bits and put in my garden. Yes, I quite like it.'

'You're welcome,' said Harry, putting the pot down on front step. 'If you change your mind make sure it goes in the green bin, not the black one. Can I smell coffee?'

'Would you like a cup?' she asked, knowing she wouldn't have to ask twice.

****

THE AFTERMATH

The CPS went along with Palmer's request and asked for suspended sentences on Riley and Burnley, and bearing in mind their admission of guilt, lack of any previous convictions and Palmer's submission as to their characters, the judge agreed and gave four years suspended to each of them.

They kept the Hanley name for the Garden Centre out of respect and made it a success.

Bloom's Centres were bought by a national chain and took the chain's name.

DS Peter Atkins was so interested by the increase in Blooms accounts he got permission to put a small team of police forensic accountants together to dig deeper and has so far recovered three and a half million from the Manchester security van robbery that had been laundered through Bloom into various offshore accounts.

Benji's rose garden was completed with lots of help from Mrs P. and very little from Palmer, although he didn't buy a padlock for the gate!

Dorothy Randall had no idea that the rose bush she nurtured in her small back garden that was so envied by her neighbours could make her very, very rich indeed.

THE END

Printed in Great Britain
by Amazon